Hexes & Hijinks
Danika Dreary Mystery
Book One

Sherry Soule

DEDICATION

To my wonderful readers,

Your enthusiasm for small-town secrets, your tolerance for my endless puns, and your willingness to suspend disbelief when my amateur sleuth just happens to stumble upon another body (*honestly, what are the odds?*) and heads fearlessly (*or impulsively? Gleefully? Recklessly?*) into danger makes this writing journey an absolute joy. And to those who take the time to leave reviews—you're the kind of plot twist I absolutely love. Your support and encouragement keeps me typing late into the night, probably consuming dangerous amounts of caffeine, but hey—what's a good mystery without a little risk? (The caffeine consumption may or may not be strictly fictional.)

HEXES & HIJINKS

CHAPTER 1

I HESITATED OUTSIDE GRANDMA ELSIE'S NEW-AGE shop, Karma Moon, my hand hovering over the doorknob and dread twisting in my gut.

After a hard jiggle of the doorknob—stubbornly locked tight—I rapped my knuckles against the door. Nothing.

Leaning in, I peered through the stained-glass window into the dark building. A neon sign—a psychic hand with stars around it—affixed to the window pitched a pink glow into the main store area.

The overcast sky darkened to a charcoal gray, the scent of pine wafting on the autumn breeze. Rain sprinkled my red Mini-Cooper snugged up to the curb, which could use a wash. I'd just driven two hours in traffic from Modesto and bug guts and bird poop had splattered the windshield.

Huh. I tugged my phone from my purse and dialed Grandma Elsie. The call went straight to an answering machine and I hung up, dropping the cell into my bag.

Was it too much to hope that Grandma had finally embraced modern technology and learned how to use a cell phone? Probably. The woman still used a rotary phone.

Main Street appeared deserted. The other businesses, antique shops, galleries, and cafes, closed and silent. Historical towns like Mystique, California shut down by nine o'clock. A touristy, mountain town so small there wasn't a mall or movie theater. Surrounding the area were gold mines, wineries, and the Sierra Foothills, a national forest that seemed to guard Mystique like a treasured secret.

I went around the corner and down a dimly lit alley. The brick building beside Karma Moon had grimy barred windows. A flickering security light over the partially open back door illuminated the entrance and shone on a planter-box with thriving greenery.

The rusty dumpster leaking unidentifiable fluid at the end of the alley banged into the wall. Startled, I yelped.

Emerging into that feeble light was a Hispanic woman. Not much makeup, nor style to her wild black hair. Her wrinkled blouse matched the color of her violet lipstick, and she had on plaid flannel pants that resembled a picnic table, with tie-dye clogs.

"Y-you startled me," I stammered, placing a hand over my thudding heart.

The woman snickered, the sound making the little hairs on my skin raise. She tightly clutched a purse in both hands, as if at any moment, it would sprout legs and run off.

I dragged in a deep, steadying breath. "The shop's closed for the night—"

"I know that, Captain Obvious." Her voice was unnaturally loud in the stillness. Then she grinned with an unsettling cheerfulness. "And sorry for the jump scare. Girl scouts honor. Cross my heart and hope to die."

An icy pressure on my neck grew colder the longer I stared at the woman. She was lying. The Crocs-wearer wasn't remorseful at all.

A slight headache bloomed behind my eyes. Just my luck—my freaky, truth-detecting psychic gift came with the worst side effect ever. Lies often felt like brain freeze, and if I caught too many fibs in one conversation? *Hello, migraine.*

She pointed a finger at me. "Ah, so you must be Danika Dreary, the flaky granddaughter that Elsie's always talking about."

"And you are?"

The woman harrumphed. "I'm Angela, her very best client. The one who's actually been here for her—unlike *you*."

Heat burned my neck, and I clenched my fists. *Ouch.* That stung more than I cared to admit.

The nerve of this woman, shaming me like that. Okay, so maybe I hadn't been around much lately, but if my grandma needed me, I was only a phone call away. We had our weekly Sunday night chats, and it was one of the few things I genuinely looked forward to. Heck, I even had her on speed dial. I called it Insta-Gram.

Angela curled her lip as if judging every particle of air surrounding me. "Where's the stick pins?" She shook her head. "Well, color me unimpressed. Clearly, you're not taking this seriously!" She darted out of the alley, the darkness swallowing her up like a frog gulping down a fly.

Stick pins? That woman was a few cards short of a tarot deck.

Shaking my head, I stepped through the open door into the storeroom, and flicked the switch to turn on the overhead light. Dusty shelves adorned one gray wall stocked with an assortment of kitschy merchandise and meditation books. The hardwood flooring showed signs of wear and warping. The room held the musty odor of an unused attic. A desktop computer, printer, and accounting ledger perched on a desk in the corner.

I shut the back door. "Nana? It's Danika."

Moving further into the room, I stood beside a gurgling water cooler near a bench backed up against the wall.

Footfalls creaked from overhead. I swiveled toward the wrought-iron spiral staircase that led to a two-bedroom apartment above Karma Moon, taking up the whole second floor.

"Hello, sweetheart." An affectionate smile graced Grandma Elsie's lips as she descended the stairs. In one fist, she clutched a rabbit's foot, her good luck talisman.

The sight of her familiar face instantly soothed my frazzled nerves. But the rabbit's foot in her hand sent a different message. Was she worried about something? Or just her usual superstitious self?

"You shouldn't leave the back door open," I said.

She glanced at the entrance and rubbed her thumb over the furry good luck charm. "I thought I'd locked it after my last client left."

I had to ask. "Matchmaking or tarot card reading?"

Grandma Elsie smirked. "A mixture of both."

While she examined the locks on the door, I looked her over. Elsie Dreary was in her early sixties, yet appeared much younger. She had short, blonde hair with soft bangs that swooped over cornflower-blue eyes and flaunted the striking symmetry of her face. I grinned at her purple fleece pajamas with a cupcake print under a plush robe and fluffy slippers. Wearing oddball PJs was one of her adorable quirks.

My own outfit wasn't quite as charming: an oversized sweater paired with black leggings and scuffed UGG boots.

Grandma Elsie faced me and we hugged. Her fragrance of gardenias and talcum powder crowded my nose and made me smile. I held her tight, feeling that sense of dread ebb away.

"I've missed you so much." She slipped the rabbit foot into her robe pocket.

"I've missed you, too."

Grandma Elsie pushed back, holding onto my upper arms and giving me a critical once-over. "Let me take a look at you." She tilted her head and squinted. "What's with the pink hair?"

Wavy pink-colored hair fell over my shoulders and framed my blue eyes and pale complexion. "It's breakup therapy. Some women go on shopping sprees, others binge on ice cream—I color my hair."

A therapist was expensive. A box of hair dye was only ten bucks.

Her grin faltered. "I knew you were wasting your life in Modesto with that jerk."

Ah, the comfort and support of loved ones. I knew coming here I was in for a lecture, I just thought I'd be able to unpack first.

My shoulders sagged. "What do you want me to say? That you were right? Fine. I guess douche-y men are my kryptonite."

Now I bet you're wondering how I ended up here.

My grand exit from Modesto had been a certified dumpster fire. First, I kneed my handsy boss in the groin after he decided my breast was company property. Even now, the memory made me want to take a scalding shower. Then, because the universe wasn't done with me, I caught my boyfriend's phone lighting up with sexy selfies—courtesy of my roommate. The grand finale? Coming home to find my belongings stuffed into my Mini-Cooper. At least they'd been thoughtful enough to pack for me.

Don't worry, I didn't key my roommate's car or sneak into my ex's apartment to swap his shampoo with hair removal, although the thought did occur to me.

With no other job prospects or places to live, I didn't have much choice in moving here. Who else would take in an unemployed, homeless thirty-three-year-old?

A sympathetic grandma, that's who.

"Oh, sweetheart." She gave me another hug before stepping back. "You okay?"

My head drooped. "Fair to partly cloudy. But seriously, I'm fine. Really," I said and meant it. My ex and I had only dated for three months so it wasn't serious, and it was the betrayal that hurt more.

"I'm sorry things didn't work out," she said. "But you should take responsibility for your life choices."

My skin flushed and I raised my head. "I know. I just need time to figure things out."

Grandma Elsie grunted. "You've been saying that for years. You quit every job you get within six months. You live a nomad existence. And you date unworthy men…Danika, I just want you to be happy."

My inability to keep a job was not a trait I was entirely proud of. I might not be happy, but I was attempting to carve out my own niche in the world. And I was still searching for my true calling—whatever that might be.

Grandma Elsie sat on the bench and patted the spot beside her. I plopped down and sighed.

She laid a hand on my arm with a twinkle in her eye. "I told you several years ago that your soulmate was out there. In fact, you're going to meet him very soon."

While I wasn't heartbroken over my recent breakup, I'd sworn not to date for at least a year. Or maybe never, ever again, you get the point.

I rolled my eyes. "No fixing me up while I'm here, okay?"

She puckered her lips. "Love is one of the greatest gifts you can receive, and I take immense pride in finding it for others."

"You would believe that," I teased. "You've been married four times!"

Her expression softened, along with her voice. "True, and your grandfather—rest his soul—was the love of my life. None of my other three husbands ever measured up, but it's high time you settled down." She sat up and narrowed her stare at me. "Danika Elizabeth Dreary, you are a smart, capable, sensitive woman. And you've always had a job at Karma Moon." She patted my knee. "Deep down, you must realize that this is where you truly belong, what you were destined to do—"

"Time out." I held up one hand. "While I'm grateful to you for taking me in, selling retail is *not* my life's ambition. But while I'm here, I'll help out."

Grandma Elsie curtly nodded. "Good. I would expect no less, and who knows? Maybe you'll find that you like working at Karma Moon."

My heart squeezed. I wasn't being very appreciative of her goodwill. No reason to tell her that I only intended to stick around long enough for my bad luck to remedy itself. And I just needed to save up enough money to live on my own and find another job. I had no plans to stay in this small town and work in retail.

My grandma got to her feet. "Let's get you settled into your old room..." Her voice faded and she froze. Her gaze widened as it roamed over the inventory lining the shelves. "Oh, no. *No!*"

"Nana? What's wrong?"

"This is bad. Very, *very* bad." Her forehead creased. "A love potion and voodoo doll are missing. Look, there's an empty space on the shelf."

She went to the storeroom shelves, frantically moving

around bottles, candles, and sticks of incense. A plume of dust rose and tickled my nose.

I fought a sneeze. "I thought those things were harmless."

"The potions are to some extent." She kept rummaging through the items. "More of the placebo effect, but anyone who steals a voodoo doll has nefarious intentions. The dolls are reserved for select clients only. "

"Any idea who might've taken them?"

Grandma Elsie paused. "Possibly a client of mine, Angela Hernández. She left just before you arrived. The poor woman is infatuated with a gentleman in town, and refuses to believe that her soulmate is not the man she's in love with."

My lips twitched. "And you know this how?"

She tapped the side of her temple with a smirk. "My psychic intuition, of course."

"Of course," I teased. "I saw Miss Sticky-Fingers outside in the alley." I briefly described the woman and our peculiar exchange, along with Angela saying the weirdness about stick pins.

Grandma Elsie pulled the robe tighter around her slender frame. "I gave Angela an afterhours tarot reading tonight because she said it was an emergency, but she wasn't happy with the outcome."

"Why would Angela take a love potion and voodoo doll?"

She raked a hand through her hair, the blonde strands standing up wildly. "I'm afraid by stealing the voodoo doll, she intends to hex the man's girlfriend, and then use the love potion on him."

"Do you want to call the police?"

Grandma Elsie shook her head. "Over two missing items? It's not worth the trouble. I'll contact Angela in the morning to sort this all out…but, ah, bad things do happen in threes."

"That's just superstitious nonsense." I placed an arm around her. "I'm sure everything will be fine."

"Maybe, but Angela is desperate, and desperate people do dangerous things."

CHAPTER 2

I BLINKED AWAKE, MOMENTARILY BAFFLED BY MY surroundings. Oh right, Grandma Elsie's. The bedroom swam into focus like a Polaroid developing: slanted wood beams overhead, beige walls with fancy molding, and enough frilly pillows to suffocate a small army. Two paintings of books with flowers hung on the wall. A cozy alcove held a huge ornate window with a cushioned window-seat decorated with shear, lavender curtains and by far my favorite part of the room—perfect for curling up with a good book or, let's be honest, scrolling mindlessly through funny cat memes.

I peeked at the bedside clock: noon. I smiled. My new boss had let me sleep in. I'd been up late unloading my car and transferring my stuff to this room.

Stretching, I got up, maneuvering around the boxes and bags, then tripped over my backpack. A pile of paperbacks poured on the floor. Crime fiction was my guilty pleasure—stories about death and mayhem, best served graveyard-col. It wasn't like I enjoyed violence, but solving the mystery and figuring out whodunit was what appealed to me.

Sleepily, I ventured into the hall and shuffled past

Grandma Elsie's empty bedroom across from mine and the bathroom. Patting my bedhead, I tried to smooth the pink tangles with my fingers.

Who needed a hairstylist when my pillow created a new hairdo every morning?

I walked into the sunny kitchen painted a bright yellow and trimmed in white, and spotted a note on the fridge: *Danika, please come down to the shop once you get up. You can start by restocking the shelves. I'm so happy that you're here!*

A glance into the living room told me not much had changed; it was still decorated in warm colors of taupe, white, and azure. A sofa with squishy cushions and festooned with a jumble of mismatched pillows, along with two overstuffed armchairs were arranged around a coffee table. Green plants in colorful pots were sprinkled throughout the space and a flat-screen TV was placed on a short bookcase in the corner, with a worn braided rug covering the polished wood parquet.

I shook my head. You know how some mornings you wake up and look forward to going to work?

Yeah, me neither.

Growing up, I'd visit my grandma every summer and during holidays. As a teen, I worked in her sweatshop while my parents dug up fossils in exotic locations.

Okay, sweatshop was a bit extra. Working at Karma Moon wasn't all that bad. While I was appreciative of a paycheck, retail was just not my jam. Though I visited Grandma Elsie every Christmas, I hadn't worked in Karma Moon in about ten years. There might be a slight learning curve.

So I had to suck it up. It wasn't like I had anywhere else to go. I could've gotten in touch with my parents, Andrea and John Dreary. They were great, if not a bit distracted and career-obsessed. My parents were dedicated archaeologists, and rarely stayed anywhere for more than a year and never owned a house.

Grandma Elsie had offered to raise me, yet my parents had declined. Thus, I grew up in boarding schools, and never had what anyone would call a real home. My dad, Grandma Elsie's son, claimed I needed a proper education. I'd gone from boarding school to a college dorm, then lived with numerous roommates over the years.

Yup, I'd been a bit of a nomad since college. Grandma Elsie has been the only constant in my life.

After eating a turkey sandwich, I showered and brushed my teeth. Since I didn't feel like unpacking, I dug through my suitcase for my work uniform: a black tank-top with the shop's logo—a pink psychic hand—and faded jeans and flip-flops. I swiped on my lucky pink lipstick and tried to convince myself I was ready to face the world of retail.

Resigned to my fate, I trudged downstairs and through the storeroom, stopping short of the closed black drapes when loud voices resounded.

I peeked through the curtains into the main store, but didn't spot anyone in my line of vision. The tangy scent of incense coiled in the air, and the space was decorated in off-white with turquoise accents and shimmery fabrics draped about. Strings of twinkle lights and dream catchers were suspended from the ceiling. The first floor consisted of three areas: the main store, a private tarot card and matchmaking room, and the storeroom.

The conversation cranked up in volume. Thrusting the curtains aside, I stamped into the main room.

No one better be messing with my grandma!

Grandma Elsie and the man that she'd been conversing with froze when I barged in. I felt underdressed compared to them. Grandma Elsie wore an eggshell cardigan sweater over a coral blouse and a chunky gold necklace, with tan capris and sensible shoes. The man was dressed in a black suit and ivory collared shirt, as if he'd just stepped from the pages of *GQ* magazine.

"Hello," I said, eyeing the tall, elegant man.

"Good morning, sweetheart. This is Ryker Van Allan," Grandma Elsie said, wringing a dusting cloth in her hands. "Ryker, this is my granddaughter, Danika."

Ryker regarded me with a shrewd gaze, so I did the same. My first impression of him was intelligence, about forty years old, and—*holy habanero sauce!*—the guy was hotter than a jalapeno burrito. Ryker had a strong jawline covered with a scruffy beard, and the kind of good-looks that made a girl want to read poetry and doodle his name in a notebook with little hearts. He was at least six-foot-two, and slender yet muscular. His smoldering brown eyes harmonized well with a straight, aristocratic nose offset by a bronze Mediterranean complexion. When a hint of a smirk touched those generous lips, the functioning part of my brain completely shorted out.

I suddenly hoped there wasn't lipstick on my teeth as I coyly flicked hair over one shoulder and tugged up the strap of my pushup bra.

Okay, yes, I was flirting a little. No judging. And I know I said I wasn't going to date for an indefinite amount of time. But...the guy was really, really cute..

"Ah, if it isn't the infamous Danika Dreary," Ryker said, his voice exuding a velvety soft tenor.

My face heated. "Oh, *no*. Please tell me that I'm not the talk of Mystique already."

Ryker softly chuckled, and the warm sound rumbled through me. "Beautiful and funny." He thrust out a hand.

The moment we touched, my heart started hammering and I hoped he didn't notice.

Ryker released me and tugged at his collar, redirecting his attention to Grandma Elsie. "Look, Mrs. Dreary, I paid five-hundred dollars for that True Love package, and the woman never showed. Nate sat in that restaurant alone for an hour. I demand a refund," he said, sounding impatient.

My psychic intuition didn't set off any alarms. He was being truthful. I knew it without a doubt.

Now I bet you're curious how I was so sure. While I didn't possess my grandma's psychic matchmaking skills, I had an extrasensory ability of a different sort. And to say it came in handy was an understatement.

Grandma Elsie paled and fanned at her face with the cloth in her left hand. "Oh, my. This has never happened before. I-I don't understand."

She swayed, and I rushed to her side. Ryker was faster and gripped her elbow.

Damn, he was quick. And chivalrous. And handsome.

Focus, Danika. Your grandmother's about to keel over.

"Are you all right, Mrs. Dreary?" Ryker asked in a gentler tone.

Pushing him aside, I grasped Grandma Elsie's arm and escorted her to a stool behind the counter. "I'll get you a glass of water."

I scampered into the storeroom to the water cooler and dispensed it into a coffee mug, then hustled back into the store. Grandma Elsie collapsed onto the stool with teary eyes. Ryker lingered on the other side of the counter. I handed her the cup and she sipped it.

This was why I was not a fan of working with the public. Some customers seemed to think a name tag came with a free pass to treat you like an emotional punching bag. Add a dash of entitlement, a sprinkle of superiority complex, and *voilà*—you've got yourself the perfect recipe for retail trauma.

"Thank you, sweetheart." Grandma Elsie set the mug down. "I'm terribly sorry for the misunderstanding, Mr. Van Allen."

"My refund?" he insisted.

I glared at the man. "Can you give her some space?"

"Let me have one more chance. I'll get in touch with the woman and find out what happened. Tell your friend to meet her again tonight at six o'clock at the Heartburn Cafe," Grandma Elsie said, her voice whispery soft. "If anything goes wrong, I'll reimburse you."

"Very well," he said. "But my friend better not get spurned again."

"You heard her," I snapped. "Now please leave."

His cheeks flushed. "I apologize. I didn't intend to..." Ryker shifted his weight, tugging at his collar again. "It was nice meeting you, Danika."

Ryker spun on his heel and left. The air seemed less dense without him.

I draped an arm around my grandma's shoulders. "You okay, Nana?"

She nodded. "I'm fine, sweetheart, simply baffled. I've never made a bad match before. Ever. I don't understand what happened."

"Was it with that woman you mentioned who stole the voodoo doll and love potion?"

"Yes, Angela Hernández, the one you bumped into in the alley. I need to call her right away." Grandma Elsie stood and rubbed her temple. After getting Angela's number from the rolodex near the shop's landline, she called the woman. "Angela, this is Elsie Dreary. I need you to meet with the gentlemen I fixed you up with this evening at six o'clock at the cafe. If you need to reschedule, please call me right away. And we need to talk. Just please call me back." She hung up.

"Voicemail?"

"Yup." She slumped back onto the stool. "This is dreadful. I wonder why Angela didn't show up. When I asked her how things went on the date, she said fine, but apparently, she'd lied to me. I-I thought that if she had the right man in her life, she'd turn things around. But I knew Angela would be a tricky one to match…"

"You've made a lot of people incredibly happy. There must be a reason Angela didn't go on the date and lied about it."

"I need to lie down, sweetheart." She got to her feet. "Thank you for looking out for me."

I laid a hand on her arm. "Sure, you're okay?"

"Only a headache. I'll be upstairs resting, and we'll have dinner together later."

"Tacos?"

She shook her head with a faint grin. "With rice and beans."

Smiling, I made a fist and pumped the air. "Yay!"

I loved tacos, any Mexican food really. If you stabbed me, I would probably bleed salsa.

Grandma Elsie vanished behind the curtains. Even with the promise of yummy tacos later, my stomach still pitched with worry. I hadn't been here twenty-four hours and already there was a matchmaking fiasco and stolen merchandise from a possible klepto.

What else could go wrong?

Wait, don't answer that. The last thing we needed was more hijinks.

A steady stream of customers flowed in after that and I was busy until six o'clock when I closed the shop. I locked up and flicked off the lights. I went upstairs and had dinner with my grandma. After reading in my room for several hours, I went to bed.

The next morning, I took a quick shower and got dressed, then headed into the kitchen. Grandma Elsie was balancing her checkbook at the table and sipping tea.

I poured a bowl of Frosted Flakes with skim milk into a bowl, then slouched at the round wooden table to eat. The table faced Main Street and had French doors that opened to a balcony. The strains of traffic and voices drifted up from the street below.

"Good morning, sweetheart. Can you go downstairs and open Karma Moon when you finish eating? I'll be down in a minute," she said.

After polishing off my breakfast, I descended the staircase to the storeroom. A piercing yowl resounded from outside. I unlocked the back door and peered into the alley.

Soft sunlight cast muted yellow light onto the body of a woman holding an empty bottle in one hand. The air stalled in my lungs. And if that wasn't bizarre enough, a fluffy gray cat was peeing in the planter-box.

CHAPTER 3

I SCREAMED, SLAPPING A HAND OVER MY MOUTH.

Can you blame me? I'd never seen a dead body before. My legs wobbled, yet I managed to remain upright.

Holy guacamole, this was not how I planned to start my day.

The body lay face up on the ground. It was Angela, wearing those tie-dye Crocs. She looked as stiff as a rusty lawn chair. Her skin was bleached of color, white foam coated her gaping mouth, and there was no mistaking the absence of life in her stare. In one hand, she clutched a red bottle.

Well, there goes my appetite for the next century. I'd seen enough crime shows to know this wasn't your average nap in a back alley. But TV did not prepare me for the smell. Or the way my stomach was doing an Olympic-level gymnastics routine.

Let me tell you, finding a dead body was definitely not in the *'How to Adult Successfully'* handbook.

The gray cat finished her business and scraped at the soil, covering her urine. She raised her head and released a loud meow.

Seriously? Even the cat was more chill about this than I was. Maybe I should take notes on feline nonchalance.

From behind me, Grandma Elsie touched my shoulder, and I flinched. "Danika? I heard you scream. What's wrong?"

Breaking out in a cold sweat, I couldn't speak. The November breeze ruffled my hair and the mid-morning sun rose higher in the sky. I moved aside so she could see the body.

And nothing says family bonding like stumbling upon a corpse together.

Grandma Elsie gasped and scurried to the woman, squatting to check her pulse. "It's Angela...she's dead," she said, standing. "Call the police."

With shaky fingers, I slipped my cell from the back pocket of my jeans and dialed emergency services. I told the dispatcher everything, gave her the address, and hung up.

"They're sending someone now. They said not to touch anything." My voice was gruff, like I'd swallowed a bed of nails.

Grandma Elsie joined me in the storeroom and we stared through the doorway at the dead woman in the alley.

The cat meandered over to us, and I crouched to stroke her soft fur. I swear she smiled up at me.

Great, now I was anthropomorphizing felines.

"What, um, do you think happened to Angela?"

"I-I'm not sure." Grandma Elsie's body trembled. "Danika, look, Angela has the stolen love potion in her hand."

I straightened, and the gray cat wound around our legs. "She has crusty foam around her lips. Could someone have tampered with the potion and poisoned her? And why's her body in the alley?"

Grandma Elsie placed an arm around me. "I have no idea, but I don't think it was a suicide. Angela was a little unbalanced, but a person with a plan. Especially, if she stole the love potion and voodoo doll."

Sirens shrieked in the distance, and the wail frazzled my already ragged nerves.

"Where did the cat come from?" I asked, my voice quivering.

"Maybe it's a stray. I'll call the animal shelter to pick it up."

I hunkered down, and the cat sniffed my hand. I checked her collar and discovered a tag with Angela's name, along with an address, and a name: *Sashay*.

Who names their cat after a runway walk? Maybe Angela watched one too many episodes of *America's Next Top Meowdel*. I'd laugh if the situation wasn't so tragic.

"She must be Angela's pet. I'll keep Sashay for now."

Grandma Elsie's forehead scrunched. "Why?"

"I don't want to take her to the shelter. It'll be traumatizing enough for the cat to lose her human, and they might euthanize her," I said and avoided looking at the body by keeping my gaze on the cat. "I guess I'll need to buy some Meow Mix."

And just like that, I'd become a foster cat mom. Talk about impulsive decisions. At least Sashay wouldn't judge me for eating tacos while binge-watching true crime shows.

"Fine, but you're responsible for the care of that animal," she said sternly. "And I warned you bad things happen in threes. This is the second one."

I wasn't superstitious like my grandma, but those missing items and finding a dead body did imply bad. I shuddered to think what number three would be.

A police vehicle came to a screeching halt at the end of the alley and two police officers hopped out. Each man wore official dark-blue uniforms with short sleeves and boots. A German Shepherd in the backseat started barking.

Sashay sprinted into the storeroom. The cat curled up in a basket on the floor crammed with clean dusting cloths, making herself right at home.

Smart cat. If I could fit in that basket, I'd be right there with her.

A cop in his mid-sixties stomped down the alley with his younger partner close behind. They stopped near the body. The dog pawed at the window left halfway down and whined.

"Quiet, Bruno!" the older cop shouted.

Bruno hung his head and lay down on the seat. I was relieved he didn't let the German Shepherd out.

Poor Bruno. He probably just wanted to help solve the case. Or maybe sniff out some snacks.

"Mrs. Dreary? Are you all right?" the elder officer asked.

"I'm fine. Thank you, Sheriff Hall," Grandma Elsie replied, although her voice cracked. "We found Angela's body and called you right away."

The younger cop eyed us suspiciously like criminals in a line-up. He was in his early forties with an ash-brown crew-cut, bushy brows, and pale blue eyes.

Did this guy practice his intimidating glare in the mirror every morning?

The older officer cleared his throat. "I'm Sheriff Robert T. Hall and this is Deputy Reid, and that's my dog, Bruno." He removed a pen and notepad from his pocket. At about five-foot eight, he had thin, grayish hair and a moustache, with a husky build and a slight belly. His skin was darkly tanned and his face craggy, like old leather boots. "Who might you be?"

"This is my granddaughter, Danika Dreary," Grandma Elsie answered. "She found Angela."

"Is that so?" Sheriff Hall gave me a critical squint. "Tell me exactly what happened."

I explained how a strange noise made me check outside, where I discovered the woman in the alley. Then Grandma Elsie told him how she heard me scream and came downstairs.

The cops knelt beside the body and examined Angela, speaking in low voices. After several minutes, the men straightened. Grandma Elsie and I listened as Deputy Reid called the coroner's office. Reid hung up and went to the car, popping the trunk lid to remove a camera. He returned and started taking pictures of the scene. When he finished snapping photos, Reid used yellow crime tape to block the alley.

Yellow tape, flashing lights, and curious onlookers. All we needed now was a film crew, and we'd have the perfect set for 'CSI: Small Town Edition.'

"I'll need statements from both of you," the sheriff said to us.

The next several hours were a blur as a forensic team of three burly men showed up. The team examined the area and dusted for fingerprints on everything in the alley. One man removed the love potion from Angela's hand and placed it in an evidence bag.

Grandma Elsie and I had our fingerprints taken. When the forensic team finished, they conversed with the cops, then left. Afterward, Deputy Reid and Sheriff Hall interrogated us inside Karma Moon. Reid ushered Grandma Elsie into the main shop, while I stayed in the storeroom with the sheriff. I sat on the bench while he paced. The water cooler gurgled, and the cat snuggled deeper into the rags.

"How did you know the deceased?" Sheriff Hall asked

I clasped my shaky hands together to stop the tremor. "I

didn't. Well, I met Angela briefly yesterday. I saw her standing near the back door last night when I arrived in town."

He wrote this in the notepad. "How well did Miss Hernández know your grandmother? Was she a friend, customer, or business partner?"

My body shivered. The storeroom felt cold and musty. I sat facing the inventory shelves crammed with dusty products. The sheriff stood in front of me.

Dusty shelves, musty air, and a looming sheriff. If this were a movie, I'd be reaching for the popcorn right about now.

"My grandma has a matchmaking business and Angela was a client." I placed my hands flat on either side of me and gripped the bench.

His hazel eyes were sharp and assessing. "What's your reason for coming to Mystique?"

"I quit my job and moved in with my grandma." My arms had goosepimples and my throat went dry. Maybe I was in shock. "Do you think this was suicide or...murder?"

"I can't officially deduce anything until we get the autopsy results back from the coroner," he said. "Do you like dogs?"

Whoa, talk about a conversational whiplash. One second we're discussing potential murder, the next it's canine appreciation hour. Was this some kind of law enforcement mind game?

My forehead crinkled. "I'm sorry. What?"

"Dogs are good judges of character. For instance, take my dog, Bruno, he can sniff out the bad seeds." Sheriff Hall scratched his cheek with the tip of the pen. "Can you account for your whereabouts over the last twenty-four hours?"

"Um, working here. I didn't even get a break all day. Then I had dinner with Grandma Elsie and went to bed."

"Do you know anyone who might have a grudge against the deceased?"

"Like I said, I didn't know her."

My blurry gaze rested on the sleeping cat. Sashay flicked her tail.

Maybe in my next life, I'll come back as a pampered feline. No job-hopping, no adulting, just naps and hairballs... no dead bodies in alleys.

"Hmm," he said, jotting down more notes. "Where was your grandmother between six o'clock and three am?"

"Home with me." My head jerked in his direction. "Why? She didn't have anything to do with this!"

"Can you or anyone else verify her whereabouts during that time? Did you ever see her leave?"

"Uh, well, no to both inquires..."

This was bad. I'd just thrown Grandma Elsie under the bus faster than you could say "family loyalty." Some granddaughter of the year I was turning out to be.

"Mrs. Dreary could've left the building unseen."

"I suppose, but c'mon. You don't seriously think my grandma poisoned that woman."

He stopped writing. "Poisoned? Why do you think that?"

"A guess," I mumbled, hanging my head and eyeing my toes. "Angela was holding an empty bottle and there was foam around her mouth." I straightened as a thought occurred to me. "Oh! I almost forgot. Two things are missing from the storeroom and we thought someone might've taken them. But Grandma Elsie didn't want to report it."

He stared at me and my body heated. Maybe I shouldn't have mentioned the stolen merchandise.

"And you say she refused to call it in?" the sheriff asked stiffly.

Oh, no. I was making Grandma Elsie look even worse. My

life was a lot like that driver who signaled right, but hooked a sharp left turn.

"It was no big deal. Only two things." I shrugged with what I hoped appeared to be casual indifference.

"Let me guess, one of the stolen items was a..." He peered through the doorway into the alley at the body. "A love potion?"

I gulped. "Yes, sir."

He stared at me until I squirmed. "Thank you for your time, Miss Dreary." He snapped the notebook shut. "If we have any further inquiries, we'll be in touch."

Grandma Elsie and the deputy returned to the storeroom. The four of us treaded into the alley, where a coroner and his assistant were placing the body in a black bag. They hoisted the bag onto a gurney and wheeled it toward a white van parked on the street.

"Wait here," Deputy Reid ordered.

The police officers joined the coroner standing near the van. They spoke quietly, and Reid shot us a scowl over his shoulder. Grandma Elsie trembled, and I wrapped my arms around her. The sheriff's German Shepherd started barking again.

Sheriff Hall stomped back over to us. "Until we can rule out foul play, including a possible homicide, this is now an official crime scene. Do not leave town. Either of you." He went back to his vehicle and got in.

The cops and coroner drove off.

Grandma Elsie's face paled as she stared at the ground. I tightened my hold on her, my own pulse skittering.

Not even 48 hours in Mystique and I was already caught up in a murder investigation. I'd need a large bowl of salsa and tortilla chips just to calm down.

You know that feeling when your life suddenly turns into a B-grade mystery movie, minus the awesome soundtrack?

Yeah, me neither—at least not until today.

Most people's biggest retail drama was dealing with expired coupons or cranky customers wanting to speak to the manager. But no, I had to level up straight to 'potential person of interest' in a homicide case my second day on the job.

And worse, the police seemed weirdly focused on Grandma Elsie. Sure, finding your matchmaking client dead in your alley with your stolen love potion didn't look great. But anyone who knew my grandmother would laugh at the idea of her hurting anyone. This was a woman who apologized to plants when she pruned them and refused to kill spiders because they might have spider families waiting for them.

Things couldn't get much worse.

CHAPTER 4

The next morning, as Grandma Elsie and I were sipping our coffee at the kitchen table, I fed the cat, Sashay, a can of tuna on a plate. It was only seven am and Karma Moon didn't open until ten.

I'm sure you're not surprised to hear that we barely slept and were still wearing our pajamas.

Since sleep evaded me, my thoughts kept drifting back to the real-life murder of Angela Hernández. Just like the opening of an Agatha Christie mystery, all I knew was that someone was dead.

The whole situation felt surreal. Every time I closed my eyes, I envisioned the body and my limbs would shake. The memory kept jumping out at me like a mugger in the darkness. I pondered the sheriff's interrogation and how he'd asked about my grandma's whereabouts.

Was she a suspect just because a woman died in the alley beside Karma Moon with a love potion in her hand?

Yeah, she very well could be.

So you understand why I had to ask. Grandma Elsie might need an alibi.

"Nana? When you went upstairs yesterday to lie down, you didn't go anywhere, did you?"

Grandma Elsie frowned. "I went to my room and took a nap. Then I got up and watched a romance on Hallmark until we had dinner together."

Truth. My built-in lie detector didn't jangle any alarms. Every lie I detected came with a physical toll—blinding migraines. It was like my body was allergic to dishonesty. Great for detecting lying liars, not so great for my social life. I mean, you try going on a first date when you can literally feel every little white lie. Talk about mood killer.

But she had no real alibi. No one who could testify that she'd never left the building.

"Who do you think killed Angela?" I asked.

"I have no idea, sweetheart."

My main concerns were these: my grandmother didn't have an air-tight alibi, we might've been the last two people to see Angela alive, and Angela was holding a bottle she had stolen from Karma Moon.

I cleared my throat that suddenly felt dry. "What about the guy she stood up? Ryker Van Allen's friend."

"Nathaniel Harrington?" She scoffed. "He's a gentle soul and a good man."

Nathaniel Harrington. I filed the name away. He was my first suspect. So, yeah, I was already planning to help solve this mystery.

"Anyone can snap and kill someone," I said. "What if it was revenge for skipping out on their date? Maybe the rejection tipped Nathaniel over the edge."

Grandma Elsie shook her head. "I really don't think he's the type. And whatever happened, my love matching intuition is on the fritz. I don't think Nathaniel and Angela were a good match after all...but there is a connection between them..."

"He might be the killer," I said. "You should tell the sheriff."

Sashay contently licked the tuna off her mouth. Someone knocked on the back entrance. The cat's ears laid back flat and her fur puffed up.

Grandma Elsie and I plodded downstairs and into the storeroom, where she unlocked the door to the alley. Sheriff Robert Hall stood in the doorway with a grim expression. The early morning sunlight shone on his badge, and my heart climbed up my throat.

Great. Just what I needed to start my day—a visit from Mystique's finest. And by finest, I mean most judgy and annoying.

"Elsie Dreary, I'm here to take you to the station," Sheriff Hall said gruffly. "You are now an official person of interest—"

"Hold up," I said, raising a hand. "The coroner has determined it's murder, for sure?"

Sheriff Hall grunted. "I can't discuss an ongoing investigation with a civilian."

"This is insane!" I said. "My grandma's not going anywhere with you."

The sheriff blew out a breath. "Relax. I only want to talk with her. We have to rule out all possible perpetrators of a crime. And Elsie might be able to shed some light on the case since she personally knew the victim."

"Oh," I said. "Why didn't you just say so."

Grandma Elsie's teary gaze caught mine. "It's all right, sweetheart. I want to help if I can."

My stomach twisted. Nana looked so small and fragile in

that moment. I wanted to wrap her in bubble wrap and hide her away from the world.

"At least let her change clothes first," I said to the sheriff.

"Be quick." He folded his arms over his chest and strode into the storeroom. "I have a conspiracy theory podcast coming on at two o'clock."

Of course he does. Because that's totally normal for a small-town sheriff. I bit back a snarky comment. Now wasn't the time to antagonize Officer Tinfoil Hat.

Grandma Elsie trudged upstairs and I followed. In the living room, we hugged, and tears lined my eyes.

I blew out a breath. "We both know you're innocent."

My grandma shook her head, as if struggling to make sense of everything. "I don't want to keep the sheriff waiting, and I might need legal advice. Can you get in touch with my lawyer?"

I scrubbed my hands over my face. "Who's that?"

"Mr. Van Allen. You met him yesterday," Grandma Elsie said. "He works next door and does loads of pro-bono work in the community. A very good catch."

I nodded and fought the urge to roll my eyes. Even with a possible murder charge hanging over her head, my grandma still thought about matchmaking.

So, the elegant man demanding a refund on his True Love package was a lawyer. Handsome, smart, and generous—Ryker Van Allen seemed to be all that and a bag of tortilla chips, too.

"Go with Sheriff Hall and answer all their questions, Nana," I said. "I'll get in touch with Ryker. Maybe see what I can find out about the friend, Nathaniel, you were setting Angela up with."

"Don't get involved, sweetheart. Let the police do their job."

"There are only two cops in this town and it can't hurt to help," I said, the gravity of the situation finally sinking in. "Besides, I need to do *something*."

And by 'something,' I mean anything to keep my mind off the fact that my sweet, cardigan-wearing grandma might be headed for the slammer. Talk about a plot twist I never saw coming.

As if I didn't have enough on my plate already with the whole adulting thing looming over me like a storm cloud.

Sashay sauntered over and rubbed against Grandma Elsie's leg. She leaned down and swooped the cat up in her arms. Sashay started purring and snuggling against her chest. Grandma Elsie kissed the cat's head and put her down. She shuffled into her bedroom to change out of her pajamas.

"I'm sorry you lost your owner," I said to the cat, then dragged a hand through my hair. "Don't worry, I'll take good care of you."

As if I had any idea how to take care of a cat. Or myself, for that matter. But hey, fake it 'til you make it, right?

Sashay meowed in distress as if she sensed the unease rolling off me. I picked her up, moved to the sofa, where I sat and placed the adorable cat on my lap. Poor thing, she'd lost her human and now I might lose my grandma on a possible murder charge. Life was like a bird. It was flying smoothly along until it pooped on your head.

And right now, it felt like I was caught in a whole flock of seagulls with serious digestive issues. Time to figure out this mess before Nana ended up trading her fluffy slippers for prison slip-ons.

Grandma Elsie returned wearing mauve pants and a light-purple blouse with loafers. "I can't find my lucky rabbit foot! I can't leave the house without my talisman." Her voice rose in pitch.

I helped her search the living room until I found it under a wrinkled magazine. "Here," I said handing the rabbit's foot to her and biting my tongue so I wouldn't chastise her silly superstitions.

"Thank goodness." She clutched it to her chest. "Remember me saying bad things always happen in threes?"

I nodded. "This is the third one. Though honestly, if the cops seriously think you're a murderer, they need their badges revoked."

She nodded, rubbing the rabbit foot in her hand. "I'd better go now."

Grandma Elsie and I went downstairs. Sheriff Hall clutched her arm and escorted her through the alley. Yellow crime scene tape still flapped in the wind. I tried not to look at the spot where Angela had spent her final moments.

My stomach did a little flip. This was real. This was happening. And I had to fix it, somehow.

I stepped outside as my grandma slid onto the backseat of the police cruiser. Our eyes met through the glass, and I waved. Sheriff Hall got in on the driver's side and started the car. His dog, Bruno, sat in the passenger-seat, his head hanging out the window. As they drove off, my heart sank.

Now I had to add 'jailbreak my grandma' to my to-do list, right between 'solve a murder' and 'figure out my hot mess of a life.'

Rushing back inside, I went upstairs to brush my hair and teeth. Then I threw on my oldest jeans, the ones with the holes in the knees that went well with my lavender tee and ankle-boots. It was only eight o'clock and Karma Moon didn't open for a couple more hours. I had plenty of time to talk with Ryker Van Allen.

Sashay pranced into the closet and returned with a ball of

socks in her mouth. Yowling, she padded over to me, dropped the socks at my feet, and leapt onto the bed.

I looked from the socks to the cat. "My feet aren't cold, but thank you for the present."

Sashay curled up inside my suitcase on top of my favorite sweater. She'd recently lost her owner and given me a gift, so I'd cut her some slack. Just this once.

Oh! I had to get a bag of cat food, a litter box, and a lint roller while I was out.

I snatched the keys off the dresser, then skedaddled downstairs, out the back door, and through the alley.

CHAPTER 5

On the sidewalk on Main Street, I paused to scrutinize Karma Moon, sandwiched between a florist and a law office. White lattice woodwork adorned the frame of the building, painted a lovely yellow, with a balcony and French doors perched above the entrance. A curving row of pine trees grew near the back of the property on a hillside. The trees were huddled close together, straight and tall, as if they were safeguarding the town.

Mystique was teeming with legendary California history. The diverse shops, boutiques, restaurants, and galleries were styled in a balance of old and new, most of the architecture still maintaining a Gold Rush façade. It almost felt like wandering onto a movie set, the buildings appeared so authentic.

"Good morning," a woman said, all bright and cheery as she passed me.

"Morning," I mumbled.

A few steps later, a couple holding hands paused in front of me. "You must be Danika. Your grandma's thrilled that you're moving here," the man said.

"Welcome to Mystique," the woman said.

"I...um, thanks," I said and kept walking.

No point in arguing with the friendly couple. Seemed I needed to have a talk with Grandma Elsie and soon. I was not staying in Mystique.

The sky was dotted with copious gray clouds shaped like puzzle pieces, reminding me I had a crime to solve. The blustery weather made the wind chimes hanging from the awning in front of Karma Moon eerily clang and whipped hair into my face. I yanked the pink strands from my eyes and tucked them behind my ears.

I located the office next door by the sign: Van Allen Law Firm. The building was two-stories and the first floor was the main workplace. I briefly wondered if Ryker lived upstairs, like we did.

Flinging open the door, I startled the receptionist. The nameplate on her desk read: Gwendolyn Chambers. On her desk was a laptop, a notebook, and a stack of folders beside a unicorn paperweight. In fact, most of the desk's surface had various unicorn knickknacks. Can you say 'unicorn fetish'? Gwendolyn even had a ceramic mug with a painted unicorn and the saying: *She is beauty, she is grace. Her horn can stab you in the face.* I would've laughed if I weren't here to keep my grandma from serving time for a crime she didn't commit.

The office was painted a pretty shade of light-blue and a single floor-to-ceiling window with the blinds drawn faced the street. The space was divided into two rooms—a closed door to an office and the lobby where the receptionist sat like a guard dog. One wall had bookshelves crammed with leather-bound law books. In the waiting area were two uncomfortable-looking chairs and a knockoff Vincent van Gogh painting.

"May I help you?" the receptionist asked.

Gwendolyn was slender and about thirty-five. Her shoulder-length auburn waves had a middle part and she wore a rayon skirt with a mauve blouse.

I wiped my sweaty palms down the thighs of my jeans. "Um, I'd like to speak with Mr. Van Allen. It's urgent."

Gwendolyn swiped a nail file off the desk and started filing her nails. "What is this pertaining to?"

"A personal matter. An urgent personal matter," I said with a touch of impatience. "Please let him know that Elsie Dreary's granddaughter, Danika, is here to see him."

She reclined in her chair and dropped the file on the desk. Gwendolyn gave me a slow once-over and her smirk implied she wasn't impressed. "Is this about that bogus love match that he bought? You owe him five-hundred bucks, you know." Her tone oozed disdain.

My neck grew hot and my hands balled into tight fists. "This is about something else. Please tell Ryker that I need to speak with him now."

"He's with a client. You'll have to wait—"

An older gentleman emerged from the adjoining office and shut the door behind him. He was at least six-three—a silver fox with shrewd hazel eyes. The man was in his late fifties and had major presence. He strode past me with barely a glance, his posture regal and his head held high, like a king among the peasants.

When the man exited the building, I looked at Gwendolyn. "Who was that?"

"You must be new in town." She snorted. "That's Gideon Harrington."

Her superior attitude was getting on my last nerve.

"Can I see Ryker now, please?"

Gwendolyn slowly scooted back her chair. She moseyed over to the closed door. I paced in the lobby, my shoulders tense. Gwendolyn knocked on the door, then opened it and stuck her head inside.

A second later, Ryker pushed past his annoying assistant. He wore a tailored, dark-blue suit and a gray button-up shirt, his facial scruff neatly trimmed. His brown eyes met mine with curiosity. My heart skipped a beat.

Well, hello there, handsome lawyer man. Was it getting hot in here, or was it just the impending doom of my grandma's arrest?

This isn't the time to get distracted by a chiseled jawline and perfectly coiffed hair. But seriously, how does he make scruff look that good?

Ryker strode closer. "What can I assist you with today, Miss Dreary? Do you need a trust drawn up or perhaps assistance with estate planning?"

My lips pulled downward. "I-I don't understand. What type of lawyer are you?"

His forehead wrinkled. "I'm an estate attorney."

Well, that was unexpected. I'd been thinking he was some hotshot defense attorney who could help get Grandma Elsie off the hook. I couldn't even manage how to find the right kind of lawyer—though in my defense, it wasn't like I had much experience with murder investigations. My expertise was more in the 'how many tacos can I eat in one sitting' department.

Shifting my weight, tears burned behind my eyes. "I thought...Oh. I think I need a criminal lawyer."

I sniffled, standing in front of Mr. Tall-Dark-and-Handsome, about to cry like a telenovela star. So much for making a good impression.

Gwendolyn scampered to her desk, never taking her eyes off us, as if this was juicy gossip she had to hear.

Ryker frowned. "Why? What's wrong?"

The last thing I need is for the town busybody to hear about Nana's predicament.

I cast a glance at nosey Gwendolyn. "Can we talk in private?"

"Of course. Step into my office."

I followed him into the adjoining room. The space reflected the rest of the office, with two bookcases, a wooden file cabinet, and a desk with a couple of leather chairs facing it. All neat and tidy. He claimed the seat behind the large mahogany desk with a laptop humming softly, and I plopped onto one of the chairs.

This office was so put-together it made me feel like a walking disaster. Did I remember to brush my hair this morning? Or was that yesterday?

"I found the body of one of my grandma's clients, Angela Hernández, in the alley between Karma Moon and your office…" I proceeded to tell him everything that happened and ended with Grandma Elsie being hauled off to the police station. "Someone killed Angela, but it wasn't my grandma."

"I don't know what to say, except I don't think Elsie is capable of murder," he said.

"Me either." I slumped in my seat. "She told me to contact you, but if you're not a criminal lawyer, then this is a waste of time. Can you refer me to someone who can help?"

"There isn't a defense attorney in Mystique. However, I can recommend one of my associates if that helps." He rummaged through some files on his desk. "I have a card here somewhere."

"Thank you." I scratched my head. My detective instincts started spinning. Angela had died in the alley between my grandma's and his business. "Did you know the victim, Angela Hernández?"

Huh. I sounded like a true investigator.

"No. Not really." Ryker pulled open a drawer and searched inside.

Maybe reading all that crime fiction was paying off. I would solve this mystery quickly and keep my grandma from going to jail.

"Can you tell me where you were last night?"

This got his attention. Ryker shut the drawer and looked up. "I was working late on a last will and testament for a client, and my receptionist, Gwen, can confirm it. Then I went out for drinks with some friends. I got home about one am and went to bed."

All true. My psychic intuition remained neutral.

Thank the tarot cards. For a second there, I thought I might have to cross "potential boyfriend" off my list of Ryker's qualities. Not that I had a list. Okay, maybe a small one

That meant Ryker couldn't possibly be the killer. He had an alibi. Which meant if he ever did ask me out on a date, I could say yes without reservation.

"Back to my grandma, do you think she needs a lawyer?"

"Not yet. The good news is, she hasn't been formally charged or arrested." Ryker stared at me balefully. "Do you have any collateral or money to pay a bail, if needed?"

I scrunched my forehead. "Ah, no. My checking account is one purchase away from an overdraft fee."

No need to mention my meager savings account, which was just several pairs of unwashed jeans that may or may not still have change in the pockets. Maybe I could offer to pay in tarot readings and crystal healing sessions?

Geez, way to adult, Danika.

"What about the shop? You could put up Karma Moon as collateral."

I slumped. "How? My grandma owns it."

"With you. You are the co-owner."

Huh. That was strange. It almost sounded like he said that I co-owned Karma Moon.

"What're you talking about?"

"You didn't know?" Ryker reclined in his chair and steepled his fingers. "Your grandmother came to see me about a year ago to update her will and she mentioned adding you to the deed on the property and the shop. I thought she told you. You are her sole beneficiary."

My jaw went slack and I shook my head to clear it. "For reals?"

Hold up. Did I just step into some alternate universe where I'm suddenly a responsible business owner? Because last time I checked, my biggest accomplishment was perfecting the art of eating nachos without spilling on my shirt.

"Your grandmother always hoped that you'd move here one day and help run the business."

My palms were slick with sweat. I co-owned Karma Moon. I owned a new-age shop. Maybe if I kept repeating it to myself, the words would sink in. I pressed a hand to my throat, suddenly finding it difficult to swallow.

Holy enchiladas, this was unexpected. I'd been plotting my escape from retail purgatory, and boom—turns out I'm actually part owner of said purgatory. Talk about your cosmic pranks.

Was this Nana's sneaky way of ensuring I'd stick around? Because if so, I had to give her props for creativity. And I thought her prowess was limited to matchmaking.

"I had no idea. That kooky, loveable old lady." My voice was raspy with emotion.

"Let me make a few calls and see what I can find out

concerning Elsie and if there are any charges being filed," Ryker said, straightening. "Try not to worry."

I wiped my palms on my jeans. "Again, thank you. Should I go to the police station?"

Ryker shook his head. "You'll just have to wait in the lobby until they finish questioning Elsie. Give me a couple of hours to see what I can find out first."

I gave him my cell number and left the office, my head still spinning. I co-owned a retail store, and I wasn't sure how I felt about that. Was Grandma Elsie trying to guilt me into staying? No, she'd never do that, but she should've told me.

The more pressing concern was who killed Angela.

CHAPTER 6

When I returned to Karma Moon after talking with Ryker, I called Keisha Gardner, an employee, to ask if she could come in today. She'd been working at Karma Moon for over three years and sounded concerned when I told her what had happened—me finding Angela's body and Grandma being interrogated at the police station.

While I waited for Keisha to arrive, I restocked merchandise. The afternoon sun slanted through the blinds over the two storefront windows and shone on the shelves outlining every wall space. When I finished stocking, I dusted the antique tables crammed with an eclectic selection of merchandise: books, gemstones, crystals, jewelry, incense, candles, and homeopathic tonics.

You might assume this was an occult shop or that my grandma was a witch, but both assumptions couldn't be further from the truth. She was a yoga-loving psychic matchmaker and a good one, too.

At least according to her Yelp reviews.

Personally, I refused her matchmaking services, preferring

to find my own dates. I know what you're thinking, after my last disastrous relationship, I evidently needed my grandma's professional advice in the soulmate department. I just wanted someone to look at me the way that I looked at tacos. Was that too much to ask? I think not.

An hour later, Keisha strolled through the door, the chill November air sweeping inside, and along with it, the aroma of damp moss and decaying pine cones from the surrounding grove of redwoods.

Keisha waved hello and made her way to the counter. "Hey, you."

I tossed aside the dusting rag onto a table. "Thanks for helping out today."

She placed her purse under the main counter on a shelf. "No problem."

Keisha and I had met many times over the years and even hung out during my summer visits. I liked Keisha and her smile was always the first thing you noticed about her, genuine with straight white teeth. Keisha was two inches taller than my five-foot-five height and she had satiny brown skin that always seemed to have a natural glow.

"Sorry to ask you to come in on your day off."

Keisha grinned. "It's cool. I'd do anything for Elsie. She's the best."

"Yeah, she certainly is."

Keisha closed the shear, light-purple curtains imprinted with silver stars that separated a small room from the main store. The private space was only used for Grandma Elsie's tarot readings and matchmaking clients.

"The police don't seriously think Elsie murdered Angela Hernández, do they?" Keisha picked up a sage bundle from the counter and lit the end with the lighter beside it. She waved the smoky stick in the air. "Because there's no way she'd ever kill anyone." She was dressed designer chic in a gray vest over a ruffled crimson blouse and jeans with low heels. The shimmery gold highlights in her ebony mane made the strands gleam and her eyes sparkled with warmth and concern.

I tucked hair behind my ears. "Did you know Angela?"

Keisha nodded. "She came in once a week for tarot readings and to consult with Elsie on her love life."

After reading dozens of mystery novels, I knew a lot of information could be revealed by scrutinizing the victim's life. If I could discover why Angela was targeted, then it should lead to the motive and the killer.

"I think Angela stole a love potion and a voodoo doll the night before she died. Those are my first clues."

"Clues?" Keisha raised an eyebrow. "Are you an amateur sleuth now?"

"Hey, I've got a stack of spy novels and enough true crime shows under my belt to at least take a shot at this. Plus, it's not like the local police are giving me warm fuzzies about their detective skills." I lifted my chin. "So about Angela—what else can you tell me?"

"Angela was completely obsessed with this dude, Patrick Hoang. I heard she'd been stalking him and harassing his girlfriend, Cassie Peters, for months. I believe in the Law of Attraction, but you can't force someone to love you."

Two more juicy suspects to add to my list.

"Maybe it was Cassie who killed Angela, it sounds as if she had a strong motive."

"Cassie and Angela were best friends in high school, but when Cassie started dating Patrick, the friendship dissolved and turned downright ugly. To make matters worse, Angela was stalking Patrick, so I'd say her former best friend was holding a serious grudge."

"If both women liked Patrick, it could have been a crime of passion."

Keisha shrugged, and roamed about waving the sage in the air, and a woodsy scent floated about the room. "How are you doing, anyway? You found the body, right? How gruesome."

I straightened a stack of books that had fallen over. "Um, yeah. It was a shock."

"Death freaks me out. I'm always scared it's infectious." Keisha pointed the sage at me. "You should add my number to your phone in case of an emergency. Just don't call me if any more dead bodies show up."

"*Please* don't put that out into the universe." I shuddered.

We exchanged numbers and I was glad to have a friend while I was here.

Keisha went about the main room brandishing the sage like a weapon. "This place needs a good smudging to cleanse the negative vibes from the recently departed. The whole incident creeps me out."

"Good idea."

Keisha left the sage smoldering in a seashell bowl, then went into the storeroom to grab more incense.

In the main store area, I meandered to a table that had bottles filled with red liquid. I grasped one and read the label: *Love Potion ~ $24.99*.

Sheesh, that was pricey. But hey, who was I to judge? I'd once spent twice that on a taco-scented candle.

Under the price were instructions: *Dab the potion onto your pulse points daily for seven days, and the potion will attract the object of your desire to you. Or you can drink it near the object of your affection, and let the magic work from the inside out.*

Fascinating. I'd always thought you had to spike the other person's beverage and not drink it yourself. Maybe that was why Angela had drunk the potion. Still, the question remained—who'd poisoned it?

I chewed my lip. Was it horrible that I was somewhat excited to solve a real-life mystery? Sure, finding a body in the alley was traumatic, but with Grandma Elsie in the hot seat, I didn't have much choice. And the local police force wasn't exactly giving me CSI vibes, so it looked like tracking down the real killer was up to me.

The bell chimed over the door, announcing customers. I fidgeted and glanced at the black drapes silently willing Keisha to return and save me from dealing with shoppers.

Ugh, retail hell. Working retail was about as appealing as eating a ghost pepper burrito. Maybe I should look for a job that didn't involve smiling at strangers and pretending to care about their crystal-induced enlightenment? I'd rather face another dead body than master the art of up-selling meditation cushions.

Considering I now apparently co-owned this spiritual shopping paradise, I better learn to embrace my internal sales guru and help people find their perfect chakra-aligning wind chimes.

Thankfully, Keisha came back just as two people wandered up to the counter. One was a guy in his early twenties, a hipster who reminded me of Shaggy from Scooby-Doo, and the other was a short, rosy-cheeked woman in her late-fifties.

"What can I do for you today, Shawn?" Keisha asked.

"I need a book on manifestation," he said.

"We have those in stock right over here." Keisha led the way across the store to a display table, and Shawn followed.

The woman walked toward the black drapes that divided the retail area from the storeroom.

"Were you looking for anything in particular?" I plastered on my best fake smile.

The woman halted and smiled. Glasses were perched on the end of her upturned nose and she wore a flower print dress and kitten heels. She had chin-length, dirty-blonde hair and a round face, with a lively gleam in her green eyes.

"I'm Lucinda Mayfair. I own Petal Pushers, the florist shop next door. I like to come by on my break and have tea with Elsie. She around?"

"She's not here today," I said. "I'm Danika, her grand—"

"Oh, I know, who you are. I'm your grandma's best friend. She's been talking nonstop about your visit for the last two days." Lucinda pointed behind the counter. "Elsie shows off your picture to everyone who enters the shop."

Hanging on the wall was a framed photo of Grandma Elsie and me several summers ago, after a hike in the woods. We were dirty, sweaty, and smiling goofily as Keisha took our picture. It had been a good day.

"It's wonderful that you're helping out Elsie. It's hard to find honest people. In fact, someone pilfered my shop last week. Can you believe it?" Lucinda shook her head. "I've never had any problems with theft before."

"A love potion and voodoo doll were stolen by a customer."

She frowned. "That's peculiar."

"Not as weird as stealing flowers from a florist."

Lucinda leaned closer and picked stray cat fur off my sleeve. "I know, it seems ridiculous. A dozen red roses were taken, along with a poisonous herb, Tanas Root."

I leaned a hip against a table and crossed my arms. "Never heard of it."

"Tanas Root is a rare plant used in small doses as a treatment for pain. I cultivate it in my greenhouse for your grandma to use in her concoctions," she said, plucking lint off my shoulder.

No wonder the cops wanted to question my grandma. A client of hers was found dead outside Karma Moon and Grandma Elsie had access to toxic plants. I knew my grandma would never purposely hurt anyone, she was all about love and positive energy. Matchmakers didn't poison their clients, they found them happiness with their true loves.

"Any idea who robbed you?" I asked.

"I think it was a former employee, Angela Hernández. She quit three days ago without notice. Like I said, it's hard to find honest help."

"You must've heard that Angela passed away," I said, my throat thick. "We found her body in the alley. It-it was terrible."

"You poor dear!" she exclaimed. "Oh, my gosh. Angela was a strange woman. Do you know how she died?"

"Poisoned, I think."

Lucinda rubbed my arm soothingly, then glanced at the clock on the wall. "Tell Elsie I stopped by. I have to go call the family and offer my condolences. Wonderful meeting you, Danika." She left the store.

It seemed Angela Hernández was shoplifting all over town. She could've been caught by someone and then poisoned. Yet that seemed an unlikely reason to commit murder. What if she stole the very thing that killed her? Perhaps Angela planned to give the poisoned potion to Patrick's girlfriend, but somehow ended up ingesting it herself.

Through the storefront window, Ryker Van Allen ambled past the shop. At the sight of him, my heart started thumping erratically. Maybe a harmless fling was the cure to a breakup. But I had no intention of staying in Mystique and starting a romantic relationship. I had plans to leave once I pinpointed the killer, and nothing was going to change my mind. Not even lovable cats or hunky lawyers that made my pulse race.

CHAPTER 7

Once Keisha's customer, Shawn, left the store, a delivery truck dropped off a shipment of essential oils and Keisha went into the storeroom to unpack the box.

A weight sat on my chest. I paced near the counter, trying to decide what I could do to help clear my grandma as a possible suspect. From the mystery books I'd read, the detective tried to eliminate all suspects so they could focus their investigation on the actual killer by decreasing the number of possibilities. My first suspect was Nathaniel Harrington, the man Grandma Elsie had matched with Angela. I would question him first and see if he had an alibi.

Before I could leave, a curvy woman in a russet wool coat with a fur-trimmed hood gave the door a hard shove. The bell above the doorway boisterously clanged as if protesting such abuse.

The thirtyish woman strolled into Karma Moon. She had dark-brown hair styled in a blunt *bob* and her face was heavily made up. Dark circles lined her caramel-brown eyes, giving off the impression that she never got enough sleep. She lifted a sage bundle off a table and sniffed it, then grimaced.

Under the fashionable jacket, the woman wore a wintergreen V-neck sweater stretched over an ample bosom, with jeans and leather boots.

Eager to help someone and get my mind off my troubles for a moment, I moved around the counter and approached her. The woman's potent perfume combined with the odor of coffee dealt a heavy punch to my sinuses.

"May I help you with something?" I asked, stepping back to take a breath of less-contaminated air.

"*Buenas tardes*." She dropped the sage on the table. "Are you new, chica?" she asked in a husky voice.

"I'm Elsie's granddaughter, Danika. And you are?"

"Sofía Hernández."

"Nice to meet you. Are you related to Angela Hernández?"

Her tired gaze sharpened. "Angela was my stepsister."

Holy guacamole. My throat constricted. For a second, we stood in uncomfortable silence. She seemed so...nonchalant. What was Sofía doing here? Shouldn't she be at home with her grieving family making funeral arrangements or next door buying flowers? Instead, she was shopping at a new-age store like nothing tragic had just happened.

Nope. Not peculiar at all.

"I'm sorry for your loss."

She nodded. "Did you know Angela?"

My nose twitched, battling the fumes. "I briefly met her once. Again, my condolences."

Sofía fingered a book on chakras. "I work over at the only insurance agency in town, if you should need anything, chica. And welcome to Mystique."

"Thanks, but I'm not staying long."

She stopped fiddling with the hardcover. "Why not?"

"Only passing through."

Her eyes glazed over like a jelly doughnut. "I wanted to leave Mystique once. Had big plans for my life, but you know how it goes, someone smothers your dreams like a pillow over the face, but now things are looking up."

I wasn't sure what to say to that. I shuffled further back from her toxic perfume to breathe easier. "What can I help you with today?"

Sofía lifted a lavender candle and examined it. "It states on the label that this candle will improve your sex life. How exactly?"

I snickered. "I suppose you light it and hope for the best?"

Sofía tittered. "People are *really* into this whole new-age movement with their vibrational frequencies, chakras, and auras." She swept a hand over a stack of paperbacks. "And these wacky books on the Law of Attraction. Such utter nonsense."

Her mocking Grandma Elsie's business made me twitchy and uncomfortable. My grin faded and I stiffened.

"There's nothing wrong with positive thinking, feeling grateful for the people and things in your life, and visualizing your goals," I said defensively.

Her lips compressed. "Whatever. I heard Angela came to see Elsie Dreary the night before she…" Sofía paused, her jaw tight. "Do you know why she was here?"

I wasn't going to volunteer any more information than I had to. Since I had no proof that Angela had stolen anything, I kept the theft to myself.

"My grandma gave her an afterhours tarot reading. She was trying to match Angela up with someone, and from what I understand, Angela wasn't interested."

Sofía set the candle down. "It's hard to believe Angela's really gone. How I used to worry about her."

An icy pressure touched my nape. She was lying. Sofía never worried about Angela. Not one little bit.

Sofía sniffled. "You have any brothers or sisters?"

"Only child."

"Lucky you. My father married Angela's mom when I was seven, a year after my real mother died. Certain men can't be alone, I guess. I would've preferred to be an only child...and I suppose I am one now." She sighed. "I was at my dad's house earlier and it's unbelievably morbid there. Maria won't stop blubbering."

We had entered the realm of way too much information. And it seemed there was some serious sibling rivalry going on. Jealous enough, perhaps, to spike a love potion with a lethal dose of poison?

I licked my lips. "Who's Maria?"

"My stepmother," Sofía said with a heavy sigh.

"Well, your sister did just die."

"*Stepsister.*" Sofía straightened up to her full five foot-one inches and stuck out her voluptuous chest. "It's no reason to blubber all day. Angela wasn't even nice to her mama. She walked all over her, treating her mama like a piece of gum stuck to her shoe." Sofía picked up a crystal and thrust it at me. "I'll take this. It says it clears negativity."

"Were you close with Angela?" I asked to make conversation and out of general nosiness.

Sofía stared off into space. Clashing emotions pursued one another across her face, as if something more complex than sorrow grappled behind her dry eyes.

"Not so much," she finally said.

I scurried behind the counter, and Sofía paused in front of it. She fingered a blue pen lying beside an order sheet. "Do you mind if I keep this?" At my headshake, Sofía picked up the pen and stuffed it inside her sweater.

Sofia was odd. She didn't seem to be grieving. And she apparently liked to keep things in her bra.

I rang up her purchase and placed the crystal into a purple bag.

Sofia leaned closer and a gust of her sickly sweet fragrance lashed me in the face. How did people not know how overpowering their perfume was?

"Are you sure," Sofia said, lowering her voice, "that you don't know why Angela came by to see your grandmother?"

Suddenly I felt like changing the subject. I couldn't tell whether she was asking out of morbid curiosity or a general interest in her stepsister's last moments on Earth. Either way, I didn't feel comfortable talking about this with a stranger.

"As far as I know, my grandma just gave her a tarot card reading." I stepped back. Another sneeze menaced my nose.

I had sympathy for the woman, but I sure wasn't going to add that my sweet grandma was a suspect in Angela's murder investigation.

Sofia thrust a hand inside the V-neck of her sweater and pulled out several hundred dollar bills from her bra. "Can you break a Benjamin? It's all I have."

"Do you normally carry around so much cash?"

She shifted her gaze. "Occasionally. Can you make change or not?"

"Sure." I took the money, gave her the change, then placed the receipt in the bag and handed it to her. "Thank you for shopping at Karma Moon."

"*Adiós*, chica." Sofia strode out the door, her viscous perfume trailing behind her like a plume of smoke tainting the air.

Sashay padded into the shop from the storeroom and meowed. I crouched to scratch behind her ears. She purred and rubbed her body against my ankles.

"You're such a good kitty," I coed.

It wasn't until I saw Sashay that I remembered she was Angela's cat. Or maybe I'd subconsciously forgotten so I could keep the cat a few more days.

Oh, no. *No, no, no.*

I could *not* form any attachments. The next time I saw Sofía, I'd tell her I had the cat and give Sashay back to the family. But then why did my heart suddenly pinch at the thought of never seeing Sashay again?

That was a worry for another day, right now I had to start my investigation.

Keisha returned to the counter and Sashay dashed into the storeroom.

"I have to talk with someone," I said, but it was more like I had a lead suspect to interrogate. "Will you be okay alone?"

"Absolutely." She raised an eyebrow. "How long you staying this time?"

Tricky question. Just the thought of living here and working in retail for the rest of my life made my skin break out in hives.

I scratched my arm. "Long enough to save enough money to get a place in San Francisco."

Right now, my bank account was pretty grim, barely enough to buy me a Caramel Frappuccino. Which reminded me to ask my grandma when payday was.

Keisha tilted her head. "You don't like working at Karma Moon?"

I threw up my hands. "Do you? You have a business degree, so why are you still here?"

"I'm saving to start a company. I want to become a life coach," Keisha said. "And Elsie gives me flexible hours."

I backed up. "That's a good reason. Um, I won't be gone

long. I want to talk to Nathaniel Harrington about his date with Angela. See what I can find out."

She shooed me with both hands. "Go. Do the sleuthing thing. I can close up the shop."

After grabbing my phone, I went through the storeroom, and out the alley door. My stare grazed the spot where Angela had died. My heart panged for the family's loss.

Once I reached the sidewalk, I paused. A police car was parked outside Petal Pushers, the florist on the other side of Karma Moon. Curious, I went inside and feigned interest in the various plants and flowers. The interior had pretty bright colors and topaz painted walls. Live flowers and household potted plants lined the wall shelves. On round tables were fresh floral arrangements and multi-colored balloons tied to two helium tanks bobbed in one corner. I took a deep breath, inhaling the aroma of greenery, roses, and glitter glue.

I had to admit that investigating a murder could be risky. But also the thought of solving the crime felt thrilling. For the first time in years, I had a purpose and it felt good.

Sheriff Hall and Deputy Reid stood in front of the glass counter, with their backs to me. My grandma's best friend, Lucinda Mayfair, was on the other side of the counter. Lucky for me there were no other customers. With my pulse thumping, I tiptoed closer to a giant vase of orchids near the sheriff, deputy, and Lucinda, and I hid behind the flowers to listen.

Fine, I was eavesdropping. You would've done the same thing.

"If you need something, it'll have to wait until tomorrow. I'm busy. I have funeral flowers to craft for Baxter's funeral," Lucinda said.

The police officers nodded solemnly. I could see all three of their profiles from my semi-hidden spot beside the counter.

"Baxter was the best hound in all the county," Deputy Reid said with a sniffle.

"A damn good dog," Sheriff Hall agreed. "But we're here on official police business, Mrs. Mayfair."

"What kind of business, gentlemen?" she asked, her eyebrows raised. "You'll need to be more specific."

"I'm sure you've heard by now that Angela Hernández is dead," Sheriff Hall said. "She used to work for you, correct?"

Lucinda nodded. "It's simply awful. I just got off the phone with her family."

"Do you know what we learned from the medical examiner, Mrs. Mayfair?" Deputy Reid asked.

I held my breath and keened my ears.

Lucinda shook her head. "Um, no. What?"

"Tanas Root. Traces of the herb were obtained from Angela Hernández's jacket, and when the corner tested it, the residue matched the toxin she'd ingested," Sheriff Hall said.

I'd been right! Angela had been poisoned.

"And since you're the only botanist we know of in town, we'd hoped you could shed some light on the case," Reid said.

Tanas Root was the same herb that Lucinda said was stolen. Coincidence? I think not.

"Of course. I grow some in my greenhouse," Lucinda said. "What did you want to know?"

The sheriff grunted. "First off, what the devil is Tanas Root?"

Lucinda faintly smiled. "An herb that contains highly toxic steroidal alkaloids. It can cause rapid cardiac failure and even death if too much is ingested."

"What else can you tell us?" the sheriff asked.

Lucinda bundled a cluster of carnations on the counter with red string. "Well, typically symptoms occur within about thirty minutes of consumption, and causes nausea, vomiting, cardiac arrhythmia, and in some cases, seizures."

All true. No cold shiver touching my spine. Yet, I inwardly trembled. What a horrible way to die.

"Why on God's green earth are you growing it?" the sheriff asked.

"In very small amounts, it also has medicinal purposes, like for pain," Lucinda said.

"In the robbery you reported," Deputy Reid replied, "I'm fairly certain that the same plant was one of the stolen goods."

She nodded. "It was, yes."

Sheriff Hall's eyes narrowed. "I'll need a list of customers who purchased this herb in the last year."

"No need," Lucinda said, "only one client bought the herb from me."

"Lemme guess..." Sheriff Hall scratched his cheek. "Elsie Dreary?"

Lucinda's eyes welled up. "Elsie would never hurt anyone. I've known the woman for over forty years, and our sons grew up together. Elsie's a good person and upstanding citizen. And she cared about Angela, more than her own family did."

All true. My skin stayed warm.

The men were quiet a moment, and the sheriff sneezed.

"Business seems slow," Deputy Reid remarked, glancing about the empty space.

"Didn't Angela's family ask you to provide the funeral with flowers?" Sheriff Hall asked.

Where was he going with this? Was Lucinda a suspect now, too? I plunked a leaf off the plant I was hiding behind to get a better view.

Lucinda huffed. "What're you implying? Florist shops have lulls like any business. It's not like I'm going around fitting people for concrete shoes or poisoning them to turn a profit," she said, sounding exasperated. "Angela used to work for me and I wanted to help her family with a ten percent discount on the funeral wreath."

"Can anyone verify your whereabouts over the last twenty-four hours?" Deputy Reid asked. "The victim's estimated time of death was sometime between six o'clock yesterday evening and three am."

She pinched the bridge of her nose. "I was working until midnight. I had a shipment of pansies and ferns arrive, and my husband came in for several hours to help me in the greenhouse out back," she said. "Then we went home. He can vouch for my whereabouts."

Lucinda was telling the truth. My skin remained warm and normal. I mentally crossed her off my suspect list. Not that I had any other leads, other than Nathaniel Harrington and Angela's stepsister, Sofia. And Patrick Hoang and Cassie Peters.

"Okay, okay," Deputy Reid said, holding up both hands. "We'll speak to your husband and let you get back to work."

The officers asked Lucinda a couple more questions, then exited the building. Since the cops didn't arrest her, they must have believed she was telling the truth. The shop phone rang and Lucinda answered it.

I waited until Lucinda strode into the backroom before leaving. But I was in for a surprise when I went outside into the bright afternoon glare. Sheriff Hall was waiting to ambush me.

CHAPTER 8

"Hello again, Danika Dreary," Sheriff Hall said.

He was leaning his butt against the police vehicle with his arms folded. Deputy Reid waited in the passenger-seat, texting on his phone. Bruno, the sheriff's German shepherd had his head hanging out the backseat window. Bruno growled when he saw me and I decided then and there that I liked cats a lot more than grumpy dogs.

"Hi...Sheriff," I said.

I started to walk past, but he pushed off the car and blocked my path.

"Why were you in the plant store?" Sheriff Hall eyed my empty hands.

Darn it. I should've bought something while I was eavesdropping. I thought fast.

"I was ordering flowers for my mother's birthday," I said. Now I'd have to actually go back and do that. I might have enough to cover a small bouquet with one of my credit cards. Sheesh, I hated being broke.

Sheriff Hall moseyed closer and Bruno barked. "You

aren't by chance snooping around a homicide investigation, are you, young lady?"

"*Me?*" I vigorously shook my head. "Nope. Just buying something nice for my mom." Sweat beaded my forehead. I was a terrible fibber.

"Uh-huh." His hazel eyes bore into my skull and he scowled.

"Are you going to arrest me? If so, then I need to set my DVR to record a Syfy movie coming on at eight," I said.

His frown deepened. "I don't appreciate your sarcasm."

"Sorry," I said. "Is my grandma still a suspect?"

"We're investigating all possible leads and persons of interest. Murders aren't solved overnight, young lady."

"Oh, I know that. Have you questioned Cassie Peters or Patrick Hoang yet? I heard Angela was stalking him. Maybe Cassie—"

"I'm not discussing the case with you. Just stay out of trouble while you're here, Danika." The sheriff went around the vehicle, hopped in, and drove off.

So the sheriff was already onto me. My heart sank into my stomach. Looking into the murder might land me in jail. But that was only if I withheld evidence or obstructed the investigation...I think. I should be free to speak to anyone I wanted to about the murder.

And I couldn't hesitate to get to the bottom of the crime. For the love of tacos, I was determined to find the killer and clear my grandma as a suspect. She'd built a life here and an honest reputation. I had to help by launching my own investigation. Plus, I found I liked having a purpose, a reason to drag my butt outta bed in the morning. Solving a mystery was even more addictive than spicy chicken taquitos.

With that in mind, I scurried along the street toward my Mini-Cooper parked by the curb. I reached the car just as

Ryker was closing the door of a silver Audi. Guess he made a decent living as a lawyer in this quintessential, small town.

"Any luck finding a criminal attorney?" I asked.

Ryker waved. He was still wearing a dark-blue three-piece suit and it looked damn good on him. "No one's gotten back to me yet, and the police are only holding your grandma for questioning. I'm sure they'll release her soon. You shouldn't need to hire a lawyer yet."

Well, attorney or not, I couldn't wait to start my own inquiry into the murder. My grandma was innocent and I vowed to prove it.

"That's a relief. Call me if you hear anything, please," I said.

"Where you off to?"

I wavered, doing mental backflips trying to decide how much to tell him. I chose to be honest.

"Nowhere special." I offered him a wide-eyed shrug, and added casually, "Just going to the Harringtons to have a chat with Nathaniel."

Ryker blinked in surprise. "Why?"

"To ask Nathaniel about his date with Angela and get his alibi." I pursued my lips. "Do you still want a refund for the matchmaking fiasco? I mean, the woman had a legit excuse for not showing up the second time."

At least Angela had seemed to die quickly, which was a small consolation for, you know, getting murdered.

"The refund can wait." He smirked. "How do you plan to gain entrance to Harrington Manor?"

"I was going to shimmy up the wall and sneak onto the property," I said snarkily. "Or I might just knock on the front door."

"It's not quite that simple." Ryker held up one hand, ticking things off with his fingers. "First off, they are a founding family, which makes them like royalty in town. Second, they live in a gated mansion with security. And thirdly, the Harringtons don't know you."

"Oh, yeah?" I placed both hands on my hips. "Well, the Drearys are a founding family, too."

What did he know? One of my great-great-great-grandfathers, a gold miner, had signed the original Mystique charter and helped build the town. So there.

Ryker checked the time on his wristwatch. "I don't have a client until this afternoon. How about I go with you? I've been friends with Nate since I moved here five years ago, and I oversee all of the family's estate planning. Although, I feel it's a waste of time. Nate's not the murdering type. The man's a pacifist."

"He still might know something that'll help catch the killer."

"I agree." He peered at me, his gaze raking over my clothes. "Is that what you're going to wear?"

I glanced down at my jeans, graphic tee with "*Books Are Better Than People*" printed on it, and sneakers. Not fancy, but it was clean. "Yeah, why?"

"With these types of people, you need to appear a bit more…sophisticated. Maybe change into a dress and heels."

I groaned, immediately dreading the thought of having to wear fancier clothing. My stomach felt bloated and my thighs were hairy. As someone who spent most of her time in sneakers, jeans, and tees, even slipping into a pair of high-heels could be challenging to my sense of comfort.

Tugging on my ear, I pouted. "*Ugh*. Do I have to?"

"You want to prove Elsie's innocence? Trust me, they won't talk to you unless you resemble one of them. I'll wait." Ryker leaned against the car and crossed his arms.

I grumbled to myself about how people shouldn't judge

you based on your style choices as I dashed back inside and upstairs to my room. Sashay dozed on the cushioned window-seat in my bedroom and peeled open one yellow eye.

"Sorry to disturb your nap," I said to the gray feline. "But when I return, I'll have a surprise for you."

In answer, a soft purr came from Sashay's throat and she went back to sleep.

From the suitcase, I dug out a baby-blue wraparound dress, my pushup bra, and a pair of strappy heels. The shoes gave me an extra inch of height and made my legs look longer than they were. I quickly shaved my thighs, touched up my makeup, and applied my signature red lipstick. After twisting my pink hair into a cute updo, I checked my reflection in the full-length mirror on the back of the closet door. Not bad for eight minutes of prepping, except for the faint circles under my eyes.

I grabbed my only decent purse, a Juicy Couture with a gold strap that I'd gotten on sale at an outlet store. When I came out of the alley, Ryker instantly straightened and whistled softly.

"It's just a dress," I muttered, and yet after putting it on, I'd hoped he would like it.

"Maybe," he said, a crooked smile touching his lips. "But you wear it exceptionally well."

My face heated. "Stop it. I have a suspect to interrogate."

Yet neither of us moved. We stared at each other for a long, tantalizing second. A hundred fantasies blossomed in my head. All of them involved him, me, and kissing. Lots of kissing.

What the jalapeno am I doing? Hadn't I'd sworn off men—or at least until I found one capable of remembering to put the toilet seat down? I shook my head, dispelling all lustful thoughts.

Now was not the time to be thinking about making out with a man I barely knew.

Ryker clicked a button on the car remote, unlocking the doors before moving to the passenger-side and opening the door for me. "Your chariot awaits."

I slid onto the smooth leather seat. The interior was clean and smelled of new car. I settled my purse on my lap and fastened my seatbelt.

"Fancy ride," I said as he claimed the driver's seat.

"Leftover from my days as a fancy lawyer." He secured his seatbelt and started the car.

"Explain," I said intrigued.

Ryker backed out and merged with the traffic. "I used to be a corporate attorney in San Francisco, where I grew up, and after eight years, I decided I needed a career change."

Apparently, the height of my own career occurred at sixteen after winning a game of Monopoly.

"How did you end up in Mystique?"

"When I was a kid, my family visited Mystique once on vacation. We did some gold mining and hiking, and I loved it. When I was ready to make a fresh start, this seemed like the perfect place to open my own law firm."

Ryker drove through an intersection and past a family strolling along Main Street eating ice cream cones.

I shook my head. "You moved to this small town on purpose? You're not under the witness protection program, are you?"

He chuckled under his breath. "I love it here. I appreciate the slower pace, the residents, and Mystique's unique history. Did you know the town was established by a man named Whitaker Mystique, who owned the sawmill where the first Mother Lode of gold was discovered in September of 1849?" Ryker glanced my way with bright eyes, and I could sense the enthusiasm in his tenor, making me smile. "Whitaker was unable to stop the surge of gold seekers flooding into the area, and decided to build the first general store and hotel. He became a wealthy man within a year without a single gold nugget, and the town grew into what it is today."

I giggled. "You must read a lot of tourist brochures."

He smiled, his brown eyes crinkling in the most charming way. "Can't a guy get excited about history?"

"I get it. You love this place. I spent summers in Mystique as a child while my parents were off on exotic adventures. I always wished I could go with them." I gritted my teeth.

Me? Bitter? *Nah.*

"Do your parents work on a cruise ship?"

I snorted. "They're archaeologists and travel the globe. You have any family here?"

"Just me." He veered left and merged with the light traffic. "My parents retired and relocated to Florida to be closer to my older brother's family and the grandkids. My dad was a former judge and my brother's a district attorney. You could say lawyering's in our blood."

I shifted to peer at his profile. "And your mom?"

"She was the chairwoman of several large charities. Now she knits, runs a weekly book club, and volunteers at an animal shelter."

"Impressive family."

Ryker nodded. "You have any brothers or sisters?"

"Nope. I don't think my parents planned to have kids—I was a happy accident," I said, saying the last two words with air quotes. "I grew up in boarding schools before going off to college. I guess, in a way, Mystique is the only real home I've ever known." I swallowed hard and gazed out the window at the buildings passing by. After a few minutes, I whispered, "I'm still kind of in shock..."

"That you co-own Karma Moon? Or that you saw a dead body? Or that your grandma is a person of interest in a murder case?"

I fidgeted in my seat. "All of the above. It's been a surreal twenty-four hours."

"And you're handling it like a champ."

Was I? I wasn't sure. On the outside, I appeared focused and determined, but my insides were twisted up in worry and doubt.

I took a deep breath and released it. "What can you tell me about Nate? Why did you contact a matchmaker to set him up on a date?"

Ryker drove onto a one-lane street. "Nate's never been married. He's sorta shy and quiet, and not real smooth with the ladies." He flashed me a flirtatious smile.

My stomach fluttered. I would not allow myself to be attracted to handsome lawyers with crooked grins. In fact, he wasn't my type at all.

Yes, you can stop sniggering now.

I snorted. "Compared to you?"

A lopsided grin appeared on those full lips. "Nate's considered the black sheep of the Harringtons. He's been groomed since birth to oversee the family's real estate holdings and other businesses, but it's not his thing. He has a degree in Art History and wants to be a teacher, but his father is opposed to that idea."

"You didn't really answer the question." I crossed my legs and yanked down the hem of my dress. "Why go to a matchmaker for your friend?"

"Nate tried online dating and mostly attracted gold-diggers. In Mystique, there's not a large pool of single women that would mind socializing with a geeky, wanna-be teacher. Anyway, I heard your grandma had an impressive success rate and I wanted to..." He cleared his throat and his neck reddened. "Wanted to help my best friend find something to smile about."

My own online dating profile would read: *I enjoy long romantic walks at sunset to the food truck for tacos.*

"That was incredibly sweet of you." I checked his hands. No rings. "What about you? Have you tried online dating? Ever been married? Kids? Girlfriend? Boyfriend? Asking for a friend."

Hang on. I couldn't get involved with the guy. My goal was to get out as soon as I could after helping the police solve the murder. Not hook up with a gorgeous lawyer. I mean, unless it was only a date or two...

Ryker glanced at me. "I was married for about three years, but things didn't work out," he said, a trace of emotion in his tone. "Currently, I have no significant other. What about you?"

All truth. I forced a tight smile, feeling pleased that he was interested. Ryker was honest and sincere, and it was refreshing. I appreciated his openness and candor. My attraction for the handsome lawyer increased by several degrees.

Oh, no. I was starting to like him. And I couldn't develop feelings for anyone in Mystique, and I didn't have much to offer a guy like him.

"Uh, well, I've never been married and I just ended a relationship, but it wasn't serious. I'm still searching for the perfect man, preferably one that doesn't make me share my nachos."

Ryker grinned at my joke.

I changed the topic back to the case I was resolute to solve. "What are the rest of the Harringtons like? I already know they're pompous." I smoothed a wrinkle in my dress.

"They come from old money. I think Nate's great-grandfather was an oil baron. Nate has a younger sister, Katherine, who runs a successful online perfume company."

Ryker drove through a secluded neighborhood on the outskirts of town into the snootiest area of Mystique. The homes became swanky mansions with increased acreage. Lots of tall trees, rosebushes, and rolling green lawns.

I rolled down my window an inch and an earthy, pine scent pervaded the interior of the car. "What does the dad do for a living?"

"Gideon Harrington is an investment banker and real estate developer. His wife, Eleanor, is what you'd call a trophy wife. She doesn't have an occupation that I know of, and then there's his mother, Blanche Harrington. They all live together on the property."

The houses grew further apart, and we drove through an area thick with majestic pine trees on either side of the road. Ryker slowed, turned onto a driveway, and stopped. We idled outside a closed gate attached to a privacy wall surrounding the property. Up a slight incline perched a huge home partially concealed by foliage and set well away from its nearest neighbors.

We'd made it to the Harrington's humble abode.

I leaned forward, peering through the windshield and gawking at the barrier. "Glad I went with your idea instead of climbing this wall."

"I would've liked to see that, especially in that dress," he said in a teasing tone. He lowered his window, pressed a button on an intercom box, and spoke into the receiver. "Ryker Van Allen here to see Nate."

A bit of static, then a male voice said, "Enter."

The huge gates slowly slid apart to allow us admittance,

and a sudden flood of nervous energy struck my system. This would all be over soon. *Huzzah!* If Nathaniel Harrington was the killer, I'd have this case wrapped up by lunch.

CHAPTER 9

Ryker drove up a winding private road past what resembled stately, park-like grounds that led to a courtyard with a marble fountain in the middle of a circular driveway. A glossy red Ferrari was parked outside and Ryker pulled in behind it, then cut the engine.

The colossal mansion loomed proudly over the property, a marvel of Victorian-Italianate craftsmanship with beautiful stained-glass windows. Boxwood hedges and colorful flowers flanked the manor. Beyond the house, the yard was woodsy and crowded with redwoods and evergreens.

Ryker got out, coming around to open my door. I emerged, trying not to gape at the exquisite surroundings.

From the side of the house, a woman in her late sixties with wrinkled skin, stood beside a willowy, older gentleman in a brown, tweed suit. He had a full gray beard, Brylcreem sheen in his hair, and a malicious glint in his shifty eyes. Cradled in one of his arms was a wicker basket with gardening tools. The man was trimming the rosebushes and she was overseeing his work.

Ryker leaned closer and whispered, "That's Malachi

Weatherby, the Harrington's majordomo. Everyone calls him Weatherby."

"Majordomo?"

"A fancy term for the chief steward of a large household. He's in charge of the estate."

The woman had short, silvery hair styled off her forehead. Her mouth was painted a dark-red and she had heavily drawn brows. A stack of pearls adorned her neck and diamonds shone in her ears. While her silk blouse had a grass stain on the hem, her linen slacks and flats appeared pristine. She reminded me of Minnie Castevet from *Rosemary's Baby*. If she offered me any roofied chocolate mousse, I was out of there faster than you could say, 'satanic cult.'

"Who's that?" I whispered.

"Blanche Harrington, the family matriarch and Nate's grandmother." He placed a gentle hand on my low-back and ushered me around the car. Then Ryker raised a hand and waved. "Hello, Mrs. Harrington. How are you today?"

Mrs. Harrington glanced up as we approached. Ryker and I stopped near the porch steps. The two of them air-kissed each other's cheeks.

"I'm splendid, darling," Mrs. Harrington said.

"Your roses are lovely," I said. "All of the grounds are beautiful."

She shrugged. "I'm a botanist. It's what I like to do in my retirement."

"You shouldn't be so modest, Mrs. Harrington," Ryker said. "Everyone knows the estate's gardens are your pride and joy."

"You're too kind, Ryker." Her hazy gray stare perused me from head-to-toe. "And who is this?"

I raised a hand and gave her a little wave. "How do you do, I'm Danika Dreary."

The woman stiffened. "Any relation to Elsie Dreary?"

"She's my grandmother."

Mrs. Harrington wrinkled her nose as if I smelled like dog poo, and her eyes became flinty and hard. "Your family is not welcome here. Please leave at once." She turned and marched up the stairs to the front door, where Weatherby opened it for her. They both went inside and shut the door.

My jaw dropped. "What the hot sauce just happened?"

Ryker scratched the slight stubble on his cheek. "Maybe she heard about Elsie being detained by the police."

I crossed my arms. "*Wow.* Talk about judgy."

Ryker shrugged. "It could be about something else. Ask your grandma, she might know."

I huffed while taking in the exquisiteness around me. Vigorous ivy scaled along the mansion's walls and manicured hedges outlined the wide porch with thick ivory columns. The heady scent of roses and fresh cut grass made my nose twitch.

Even though, the impolite woman had told me to leave, I didn't want to. I had read enough whodunnits to know that I couldn't give up just yet.

I kicked at the ground with the point of my heel. "Can you go inside and ask Nate to come out?"

"Sure thing." Ryker lightly touched my elbow. "Wait here. No snooping around the mansion for clues. I'll be right back." He dashed into the house.

I leaned against the Audi and sulked. Even my posh clothing hadn't helped me gain any favor with the snobby Harringtons. And what was the source of this inexplicable grudge against my family, you might ask? I hadn't a clue, but I was going to find out.

Ryker returned with a man in his early thirties, who had to be Nate. The guy had a close-shaven beard, curly golden-brown hair, and wore round-framed glasses. He resembled a hip high school teacher in a button-down shirt and khaki pants with leather loafers. His socks peeping out from the hem of his pants were mismatched, one a dark purple and the other a soft blue.

Nate smiled cordially as he advanced with his hand out. His handshake felt timid and he seemed like the conservative, country club type, hardly murderous, perhaps even meek. But under that preppy attire might lurk the cold-heartedness of a killer.

"Nate," Ryker said. "This is Danika Dreary."

"Hello," Nate said to me, and then looked to Ryker with a grin, like an eager kid on a play date.

"I wanted to ask you a few questions if you don't mind," I said. "First, do you know why your grandmother just snubbed me? What's that all about?"

Nate's attention returned to me. "Sorry about that. She's just not comfortable with newcomers or anyone outside her social circle."

It wasn't a real answer, but it wasn't that important right now anyway. I let it go.

"You might already be aware that Angela Hernández's body was found near our shop..." I paused, surprised I'd use the word *our*.

"Yeah, I heard. It's tragic." Nate scrubbed a hand over his face.

"You were supposed to meet Angela for a dinner date," Ryker said.

"Which time? She stood me up twice." Nate's throat worked. "The second time, I waited at the Heartburn Café, but she never came, so then I went home. I feel like a jerk for being irritated now that I know she's dead."

My neck stayed warm. Truth.

"How well did you know Angela prior to being set up on the date?" Ryker asked.

A muscle ticked along Nate's jaw. "I saw her once or twice here at the house, and besides saying hello as we passed each other in the kitchen, we never spoke."

"Wait, what?" I said confused. "Why would she be at your house?"

"Angela's mother, Maria, works for us as a housekeeper, and occasionally Angela came by to visit her," Nate said, straightening his glasses. "I was disappointed that Angela had no-showed again."

A tingle of coldness slapped my nape. A lie. He wasn't disappointed at all.

I wished I could just blurt out that I knew he was lying, but knowing someone's lying isn't the same as knowing *why* they're lying. For all I knew, Nate could be covering up embarrassment rather than murder. Plus, the moment I started throwing accusations around, people's mental defenses went up faster than rent prices in San Francisco. Their walls blocked my ability like spiritual noise-canceling headphones.

No, if I wanted to get to the truth, I had to be sneaky about it. Besides, I needed actual evidence, like a confession, not psychic hunches.

"*Really?*" I said, eyeing him closely. "So you thought maybe there was a chance there could've been a spark between you two? And when Angela stood you up, maybe you got angry..." I let the implication dangle in the air between us.

"And murdered her?" Nate blinked, as if hearing this accusation had startled him awake. "*No!* I was only distraught to discover the potential love of my life was dead."

My intuition was shrieking like a wailing banshee. The chilly sensation spread to my shoulders, freezing my skin.

"You're lying," I accused.

Nate's eyes widened. "Why would you say that?"

"Because you are. I know it," I blurted without thinking.

Oh, holy hot sauce. I'd just broken the cardinal rule of having a secret psychic ability—*don't tell people you have a secret psychic ability!* My mouth had gotten ahead of my brain, like a runaway food truck with no brakes. I needed to backpedal. Fast.

But how do you un-accuse someone of lying without making yourself look completely bananas? This was definitely not covered in any of my previous job trainings—though to be fair, most jobs didn't require expertise in psychic damage control.

Nate stared at me, as if waiting for an explanation. The silence stretched like melted cheese, and not in a good way.

Finally, Nate rubbed the back of his neck with one hand. "All I know is that Angela worked as a cashier at Petal Pushers and she seemed like a pleasant woman."

"Did Angela's mother know about the date?" Ryker asked. "Did your family?"

"I have no idea if Angela's family knew, but my sister, Katherine, did." Nate cleared his throat. "She accused me of dating below our station, like we live in the Victorian era."

"And do you mind telling us where were you last night?" I asked.

Nate glanced at Ryker, then me. "I was at the café waiting for Angela, and she never showed."

Truth. No cold tingles on my skin that said otherwise.

I placed a hand on my hip. "How long were you there, Nate?"

"About two hours from five until seven." He took off his

glasses and cleaned the lens on his sleeve, then slipped them back on. "Before that, I spent the day at my father's office filing paperwork. About a dozen employees can verify my whereabouts."

My nape warmed. Honesty. Damn. He might have an alibi. I tried not to act too disappointed. And yet, he had also lied, which meant he was either covering for someone or withholding information about the crime.

A police cruiser drove up and parked behind the Audi. Sheriff Hall and Deputy Reid got out, the engine still running, and approached us. The sheriff's eyes enlarged as if surprised to see me.

"Nathaniel Harrington," Sheriff Hall said, "I need you to come down to the station, please."

Sweat dotted Nate's forehead, and Ryker's brows furrowed. I sucked in a soft breath.

Did the sheriff have evidence against Nate? Was Grandma Elsie free of blame now? Maybe I was right! Ryker's best friend might actually be the killer.

"Why?" Ryker asked, moving in front of Nate.

"It's concerning the death of Angela Hernández," Deputy Reid replied. "Now move aside."

"It's okay, Ryker. You're an estate attorney, not a criminal lawyer, and I want to help," Nate said before facing the sheriff. "Can I take my own car?"

"I think it might be best if you rode with us," Sheriff Hall said.

The door to the house flung open and Gideon Harrington, Nate's dad, emerged. I'd forgotten how tall he was when I'd last seen him at Ryker's office, the silver fox was well over six-feet tall and wore a white collared-shirt with black slacks. Gideon's stare honed in on the five of us standing in the courtyard.

"Nate! Don't say a word until I arrive with our lawyer," Gideon said, rushing down the porch steps. "I'll be right behind you, son." He charged around the side of the house to the garage.

The cops and Nate got into the police cruiser. With frustration, I watched the car drive off with my prime suspect.

CHAPTER 10

Ryker and I got into his car parked in the circular driveway of the Harrington estate. He stared out the window. Gideon Harrington zoomed past us in a green Mercedes and tore down the driveway, kicking up gravel.

I touched Ryker's arm. "You okay?"

He was quiet, then jammed the key into the ignition. "Nate didn't do this." His voice sounded strained.

"He wasn't charged with anything. The police only want to talk to him."

From a window on the second floor of the mansion, someone was holding the curtains apart and peering out. The afternoon sunlight glinted off the glass. I leaned closer and squinted through the windshield. The person dropped the drapes. Maybe it was Mrs. Harrington making sure I left the premises.

"I guess I should go home and wait for my grandma," I said.

"You wanna grab lunch first? We can go over what we know about the case." His lips twitched as he eyed me from head-to-toe. "Besides, we can't let that pretty dress go to waste."

I blushed. "You want to help solve the murder? Why?"

"I'm worried about my best friend." Ryker's knuckles, turned white as he gripped the steering wheel. "Elsie and Nate are innocent, and we should work together on this. I can't let Nate go down for a crime he didn't commit because of a date I set him up on. I just wanted him to meet a nice girl, not go to prison for her murder."

Except his best buddy was a liar. While I didn't like implicating Nate without definite proof, I had to trust my instincts.

"Okay, let's go to the Heartburn Café," I said.

"Sounds good. I'm starving."

Ryker and I were both quiet on the drive to the restaurant, lost in our own thoughts of whodunit and why. My mind spun with questions. Was someone trying to frame my grandma? Or possibly Nate? I wondered if Nate really sat alone waiting for Angela in the cafe. Maybe the staff could verify it. I would ask them while we were there.

He parked in front of the Heartburn Café, a charming restaurant with a white and red striped awning. Two huge windows flanked the glass door. A trendy chalkboard sign with specials written on it stood on the sidewalk.

When I walked inside, the aroma of spices, fresh baked bread, and garlic made my mouth hyper-salivate. The place wasn't crowded and had a cheery ambiance, with soft guitar music playing in the background. Ryker and I claimed seats by one of the windows facing Main Street, him on one side of the table and me on the other. Salt and pepper shakers were placed on the table beside a napkin dispenser and a container jammed with sugar packets.

A waitress came by and set a basket of bread and two waters on the table. "I'll be right back to take your order," she said and was gone in a flash to wait on another customer.

I grasped a sugar packet and fiddled with it. "I know he's your best friend, but Nate lied to us."

If only it was as simple as just asking someone if they killed Angela, but my gift wasn't a foolproof lie indicator. People who convinced themselves of their own innocence wouldn't trigger it, and the truly guilty rarely gave straight answers. No, I'd need to be smarter about this.

"What makes you think that?" He shrugged off his suit jacket to reveal a long-sleeved, button-up shirt.

How did I respond without him thinking I was a weirdo? Ignoring it for now seemed like the best option.

I put the packet back into the container. "Any idea what he was trying to hide?"

He seized a roll and pointed it at me. "Not a clue. You didn't answer my question."

I searched for the waitress. Wasn't someone going to take our order? Save me from answering?

Come on, universe. Throw me a bone here. A spontaneous dance number. An impromptu fire drill. Anything!

"You can trust me, you know," he said quietly.

I stared into those brown eyes and knew I could. Though I rarely told anyone about my special ability, I wanted to trust Ryker. Grandma Elsie obviously did, so I should, too. Still, I couldn't meet his eyes. My body stiffened and I reached for a napkin. I unfolded it and refolded it into smaller squares.

Time to reveal my freak flag and hope he doesn't run screaming for the hills.

"When I was a child, I realized I could tell whenever someone was lying," I said, checking to make sure our conversation was private. "I'd feel a cold sensation on the back of my neck. The colder it got, the bigger the lie. My grandma has psychic intuition too and that's how she matches people up. And when my dad touches artifacts, he says he gets visions of the past, which must come in handy being an archeologist. Different types of psychic abilities run in my family."

Ryker rested his forearms on the table and leaned closer, lowering his voice. "That's quite intriguing."

I couldn't tell whether he was being serious or snarky.

"When I was seven, I caught my mom lying to my dad about having a secret savings account that he didn't know about. As an adult I get it now, my dad's a spender and she'd rather save money. At first, she thought I was only perceptive and interpreting people's body language, then my parents realized I had a unique gift..." I stopped rambling. Ryker's expression was blank. "Oh, boy. I hope I haven't freaked you out by oversharing."

Ryker placed a hand over mine. Our gazes clung and my heartbeat sped up. His expression was sympathetic and thoughtful.

"I think you're extraordinary," he said after a few seconds had gone by.

My heart fluttered in my chest and the tension in my body eased.

His gaze brightened. "You have an amazing gift," Ryker said. "Man, I could've used you in the courtroom."

We both laughed.

"Why'd you quit practicing corporate law?"

He cleared his throat. "I became jaded by all the shady dealings and cover-ups behind the scenes. My conscience got the better of me, and one day, I woke up with a pit of dread in my stomach. I couldn't do it any longer, so I quit and moved to Mystique. I've never looked back."

"And you're happier now?"

"I love it here. No traffic or smog, and no one's in a rush. Doing estate planning is a welcome change of pace. What about you?"

I hesitated, not wanting to sound like a total loser. "Um, it's not that I hate Mystique. When you lose your boyfriend, apartment, and job in one day of high drama, you learn to be grateful for whatever life throws your way."

And at least Grandma Elsie didn't make me sleep in my Mini-Cooper.

He sat back. "Seriously? How did that happen?"

I told him all about my ex cheating on me with my roommate and my pervert boss. "I called my grandma and she told me to come home. She's been my rock my whole life, the only person I can count on…" My voice died and tears stung my eyes. "I have to prove her innocence. She's always been there for me and I owe her no less."

"I'll do whatever I can to help," he said in a soothing tone. "Elsie is good people."

"She is…did you ever hire my grandma for a match?"

He snickered. "I don't need a matchmaker to get a date." Ryker flashed me a crooked smile that faded as quickly as it appeared. "However, your grandma did tell me that I was going to meet someone very special."

Hmmm. She'd told me the same thing the night I'd arrived. I changed the topic.

"Nate said his sister, Katherine, wasn't happy about him going on a date with the housekeeper's daughter. What's Katherine like?"

Ryker shrugged. "She's okay."

"What does that mean? You gotta give me more than 'she's okay.' What type of person is she?"

He hesitated and averted his stare. "If you're alluding to Katherine being a murderer, I doubt it."

"How well do you know her?"

Ryker took a long gulp of water before answering, as if he was suddenly dying of thirst. "Pretty well."

"Ryker, what's up with you?" Then it dawned on me. "You used to date her."

His cheeks tinged pink. "Only for a couple of months. That's how I met Nate."

"Why'd you guys break up? Does she snore? Eat with her mouth open? Snort laugh?"

Ryker tugged at his collar. "Katherine's a workaholic and always attending some gala, charity event, or business dinner. That's just not my scene anymore."

"So Katherine wasn't into chilling at home with a glass of pinot grigio, a plate of nachos, and watching Netflix?"

"Not at all. I left Katherine's lifestyle behind when I moved to Mystique. The one good thing that came out it is now I know exactly what I want and what I don't want in a relationship." Those flawlessly shaped lips curved into a heart-melting grin. He stretched out a hand and laced our fingers. "I know it might sound strange, but I'm glad we hung out today. I just wish it was under different circumstances."

His fingers tightened on mine. My heart skipped a beat. I suddenly wondered what it would feel like to be held in his arms. His eyes brightened as if he were imagining the same thing. My breathing sped up. Someone chortled and he released his hold.

Ryker leaned back in his chair. "So, what do you want to order?"

I quirked an eyebrow. "Hmm, probably the jalapeño poppers to start. Spicy, cheesy, and wrapped in bacon. What's not to love?"

"Good choice."

I tapped my finger on the menu. "And what about you, counselor? Let me guess...the pretentious filet mignon?"

Ryker clutched his chest in mock offense. "Ouch! I'll have you know I'm more of a comfort food guy. Give me a good old-fashioned cheeseburger any day."

"Really? I pegged you for caviar and champagne."

"That was the old Ryker. New Ryker prefers beer and nachos." Ryker leaned forward, resting his elbows on the table. "So, what's the weirdest job you've had? Your grandmother mentioned something about a rather diverse resume."

I rolled my eyes, twisting a lock of pink hair. "Um, where do I even start? Though I guess being a professional dog walker for hyper breeds was the hardest. Imagine getting dragged through around by six huskies who thought they were training for a sled dog race."

"That sounds exhausting," Ryker said with a grin. "I bet you were in great shape, though."

"Oh yeah, my calves were rock solid. But the worst job of my career? Being a party entertainer dressed as a taco. And before you ask—yes, there are photos, and no, you can't see them."

He chuckled, and I tried not to notice how the sound made my stomach do a little flip. I studied his face, noticing the tiny laugh lines around his mouth and the warmth in his gaze.

"My career's been strictly courtroom drama," he said. "Though I did once watch a judge doze off during a boring tax fraud case. The bailiff's snoring was the most exciting part of the trial."

The waitress came by and took our orders, a burger and fries for him and a pasta salad for me.

"Do you have any photos of Nate on your phone?" I asked, sipping my water. "I want to check his alibi."

Ryker reached into his pocket and removed his cell. He scrolled through the photos, stopped on one, and handed me the phone.

"Thanks. I'll be right back."

Taking the cell with me, I went to the kitchen area and asked several employees if they'd seen Nate here the night Angela died. A few said they had and that Nate had sat alone for hours.

One of the waiters scratched his unshaven cheek. He was short with a reddish mop of hair and boyish good-looks. "I remember him. Attractive guy and a big tipper. I felt bad for him because it was obvious he'd been stood up. Is he, uh, still single?"

"I don't think he's gay."

The waiter smirked. "You sure about that?"

"Well, no."

"I'm only working here part-time while I'm in college. My name's James, and I'm majoring in computer science, you know, if you should see him again."

I nodded. "Got it. I'll let him know a future computer tech has the hots for him. And if you want to meet eligible singles, my grandma has a renowned matchmaking service at Karma Moon."

"Thanks." James left to wipe down a table.

Well, it seemed that Nate had a solid alibi, which demolished my theory of him being the killer. I returned to the table, retook my seat, and gave Ryker back his phone.

"Nate was telling the truth, he was here."

Ryker blinked. "I hope you're done trying to blame an innocent man."

"I am, but remember my psychic superpower? Well, it's never wrong, and Nate is still hiding something. But I'll admit, I don't get a murderous vibe from your best friend."

The waitress appeared with our food and we chatted while we ate. My meal was delicious, and I wiped my mouth with the napkin when I'd finished. The waitress set the check on the table. Ryker insisted on paying, and I thanked him for lunch.

While we waited for the waitress to return with his credit card, a woman with freckled skin and a shrewd gaze stalked over to our table.

CHAPTER 11

The woman paused beside Ryker and he stiffened. She reeked of money—Chanel N°5 and a limitless gold card. She was thirty-ish and as beautiful as a cold, uncut diamond. She had natural red hair and wore a long-sleeved cashmere sweater, with designer jeans and soft leather boots that probably cost more than my Mini-Cooper.

"Greetings, Ryker," she said, ignoring me.

"Hello, Katherine. This is Danika Dreary." He gestured to me. "This is Katherine Harrington, Nate's sister."

"Hi," I said meekly.

"Heard you were at the house earlier." Katherine flicked a glance in my direction. "Grandmother was quite distressed by your visit."

I grimaced. "Sorry about that. Do you know why she got so upset?"

"You don't?" She snickered. "I would ask your grandmother. There's been bad blood between our families for years." She smiled at Ryker and ran her hand over his shoulder. "We should do dinner this week."

Oh, barf. Could she be any more obvious? I fought the urge to gag.

He detached her hand. "I don't think that's a good idea."

"Don't be like that," she purred. "Remember that night we spent at the beach house—"

"May I ask you a question, Katherine?" I said, interrupting her gross trip down romance lane. I did not want to listen to them reminiscing about their past love life. "About Angela Hernández."

Her nostrils flared. "Our housekeeper's daughter? What about her?"

I leaned forward and lowered my voice. "She died outside our, I mean, my grandma's store."

Katherine frowned, but it didn't extend to her unlined, Botoxed forehead. "What's that got to do with me?"

"Nate said you weren't thrilled about him dating Angela," Ryker said. "Can you tell us why?"

"Angela was a cashier at a florist," Katherine said with a haughty sniff. "Besides, she wouldn't last ten seconds in our world. I was only looking out for my brother and saving that poor woman from heartache and humiliation. The Harringtons don't fraternize with the help."

Wow. Talk about a world-class snob.

"When was the last time you saw or spoke to Angela?" Ryker asked.

Katherine's lips puckered. "I run into Angela at the hair salon, and advised her not to date my brother. Fortunately, Angela said she had no intention of going to dinner with him. We parted ways and I was relieved that I didn't have to bribe the little gold digger."

My jaw dropped open. "That was a joke, right? You wouldn't really pay someone not to date your brother."

She deadpanned. "Of course, I would."

How could Ryker have dated a woman like Katherine? She was so snooty and arrogant.

I shifted in my seat and narrowed my gaze. "Where were you last night?"

Katherine shifted closer to Ryker's chair. "Why? Do you work with the police?"

"I think what Danika's trying to ask is," Ryker said, "do you have an alibi for your whereabouts the night Angela died?"

"How dare you go around accusing people of murder," Katherine grumbled.

"We only want to rule out anyone who knew Angela," I said. "The police will probably ask you the same questions since Angela's mother is your housekeeper."

"Well, if you must know, I was meeting a potential investor at Brewed Awakening for coffee," Katherine said, flicking her crimson tresses over her shoulder.

Lie. A frosty chill numbed my neck. Her alibi was as slick and icy as a skating rink. I wasn't sure I could call her out on it without explaining how I knew she was lying. Ugh, being a human lie detector was such a pain sometimes. I wished my psychic-ness came with a built-in printout—that would be more convincing than saying my spidey sense was tingling.

And I couldn't just blurt out, '*Hey, did you kill anyone lately?*' Because clever liars could just think about that one time they didn't murder someone and technically not be lying. Subtlety was key, even if subtlety and I weren't exactly BFFs.

"The person you should be interrogating is Cassie Peters, Angela's former best friend. Everyone knows Angela was pursuing Cassie's boyfriend."

Hmmm. A spurned and jealous ex-best friend. Sounded promising.

"Thanks for the tip. I'll talk to Cassie," I said.

Ryker titled his head. "Did you ever get that loan to expand your business, Katherine?"

Katherine leaned closer to Ryker, her perfume wafting through the air. "Other resources, darling. I have my ways." She winked, her fingers brushing his arm.

I gritted my teeth, fighting the urge to roll my eyes. The Heartburn Cafe suddenly felt too small, too stuffy. Maybe I could ask the waiter to turn up the AC. Or dump a bucket of ice water on Katherine's head. You know, for the greater good.

"Oh, Ryker," Katherine purred, "remember that little bistro in San Francisco? The one with the to-die-for tiramisu?" She leaned closer to Ryker, batting her mascara-coated eyelashes. "We should go there again sometime, for old time's sake."

Ryker shifted in his seat, clearing his throat. "Ah, well, that was a long time ago, Katherine."

My stomach churned. I mean, sure, I had no claim on Ryker, but watching a murder suspect try to seduce him made me want to dump a whole bottle of hot sauce in her designer purse.

I took a sip of my water, crunching loudly on an ice cube. The cheerful chatter of other diners faded into white noise. I focused on not throwing my glass at Katherine's perfectly coiffed head.

"Nonsense," Katherine chirped, her hand now resting on Ryker's shoulder. "It feels like yesterday. Don't you miss those days, darling?"

I couldn't take it anymore. "So, Katherine," I interrupted, my voice syrupy sweet, "about that investor meeting. Did you actually get the funding you needed? You never really said."

Her smile faltered for a moment before regaining its

megawatt brightness. "Oh, sweetie, that's not really your concern, is it?" She patted my hand condescendingly. "Leave the business talk to the grown-ups."

Ryker frowned. "Now, Katherine, that's uncalled for. Danika's just trying to help with the investigation."

"*Please.* I've heard all about you, Danika." Katherine scoffed, her laugh tinkling like broken glass. "As if this drifter could solve anything more complex than a missing sock mystery."

The comment hit a nerve. Okay, *fine*—maybe my life was more food truck than five-star restaurant, moving from job to job and place to place. But my intuition told me Miss Perfect's carefully crafted image was about as genuine as gas station guacamole.

I leaned forward. "At least I'm not lying about my whereabouts on the night of a murder."

Katherine's face paled. "Excuse me?" she hissed, her composure cracking.

Ryker's gaze darted between us. "Danika, what are you talking about?"

I took a deep breath, the scent of coffee and grilled sandwiches filling my lungs. "Your alibi, Katherine. It's as fake as your eyelashes."

Katherine sneered. "Oh, sweetie, is this about the crush you have on Ryker? How...quaint. I suppose I can't blame you for trying to get his attention." She patted Ryker's shoulder. "I have to go. We'll do dinner. Somewhere with more...sophisticated company."

Katherine shot me a withering glare before she strutted to the counter, grabbed a takeout bag, and proceeded out the door.

I watched her leave, fighting the urge to stick out my tongue at her back like a mature adult. Katherine might think the Harringtons owned this town, but from what I'd learned about Angela, she couldn't have cared less about their family's social status. And she was the second person to mention Cassie Peters and Patrick Hoang. Angela seemed to have made a lot of enemies in Mystique.

We left and Ryker drove me to Karma Moon. He parked and opened the car door. The cerulean sky had a string of lazy clouds and a crisp breeze tousled the branches on the maple trees lining the street.

Ryker clasped my hand and escorted me to the back door. His touch made my heart do a big drum solo. His shoulder brushed mine and his scent struck my senses, a smoky blend of apples, bergamot, and leather. Ryker paused outside the door and untangled our fingers. For a wild moment, I thought he might kiss me. Instead, he only smiled down at me.

No smooches for Danika. Yeah, I was disappointed, too.

"You should put my number in your phone," he said.

I handed him my phone, and he added his number to my contacts. Taking it back, I slipped it into my purse.

"I'm sorry, Ryker. I know she's your ex, but... Katherine was lying about her alibi. I can feel it."

He ran a hand through his hair, sighing heavily. "You can't just accuse people without proof, Danika."

"I know, I know. Just trust me, she's not telling the truth about where she was that night."

Ryker studied me for a long moment, his brown eyes searching mine. "All right, let's say you're right. What's our next move?"

I blinked, surprised by his sudden shift. "You believe me?"

He nodded. "I want to trust your hunches. But we need real evidence, Danika. We can't build a case on your cold neck tingles."

"You're right—we need something more solid than my weird psychic vibes."

"Okay, so then we can do more sleuthing tomorrow." He ambled back to the Audi.

Instead of going inside, I hopped into my car and drove to Furbabies-R-Us, a business that had a variety of pet supplies, animal provisions, and veterinary services. Using my 'in-case-of-emergency' credit card, I left with everything a spoiled cat could possibly need.

I might've overspent. It wasn't like I could keep Sashay. She belonged to Angela's family and I couldn't take a cat with me when I left, right?

Oh, stop shaking your head at me.

Back at Karma Moon, I unlocked the back door.

Creaking footsteps from the apartment above made me freeze in the storeroom. My heart thumped as I tiptoed up the spiral staircase.

CHAPTER 12

I WENT UPSTAIRS AND FOUND GRANDMA ELSIE lounging on the couch and cradling a bowl of popcorn while watching a *Lifetime* thriller. Sashay snoozed on the overstuffed armchair. My heart swelled at the sight of my grandma.

"You're back!" I exclaimed, tears clouding my vision.

I dropped the cat stuff I'd bought on the floor and rushed across the room. "I was worried about you, Nana! I need a hug."

She stood, set the bowl aside, and we embraced. She looked comfy in light-blue pajamas adorned with yellow ducks and thick socks. Her fluffy, blonde tresses framed her makeup-less face.

"How did you get home?" I asked, moving out of her arms. "And where did you get those *kuh-razy* cute PJs?"

Grandma Elsie tittered, retaking her seat and reclaiming the popcorn. "Sheriff Hall said he didn't have enough evidence to officially charge me with anything. However, he let me go on the condition that I don't leave town. I'm sure the real killer will be apprehended soon enough and locked up in the slammer." She popped a kernel into her mouth and winked. "The pajamas I bought at Kohl's."

"You're putting a lot of faith in this two cop town." I plopped next to her and grabbed a handful of popcorn. "Why didn't you call me to pick you up?"

"The deputy gave me a ride home. On the way, I saw you through the window having lunch with Ryker." Her face lit up. "Tell me *everything*. How was your date?"

"It wasn't a date, Nana." I dropped three buttery kernels into my mouth.

"Did he pay for the meal?"

I swallowed. "Well, yes."

"Then it was a date." Grandma Elsie blew out a breath and stared at me levelly. "You do like him, don't you?"

The heater kicked on and rumbled the pipes. Warm air circulated through the vents into the room.

I sighed. "Ryker's charming, but romance is the last thing on my mind. You sure you're okay?"

Grandma Elsie waved off my polite concern. "Of course, sweetheart, I can take care of myself." She patted my hand. "I did just survive a stretch in the county bed and breakfast."

"Will you get serious?" Giggling, I grabbed the remote and lowered the volume. "How did it go? The questioning?"

"It was pretty routine. They asked about Angela, her life, and our relationship. I answered honestly and I think the sheriff believed me, but Deputy Reid was a tad uncouth."

I nodded, my mind drifting to the Harringtons. Talk about uncouth. Katherine's icy glare could've frozen Hell over, and don't even get me started on Blanche's sneer. I wasn't exactly Miss Congeniality, but their hostility seemed way over the top.

"I need to ask you something." I proceeded to tell her about my encounters with Blanche and Katherine Harrington. "I get the feeling their rudeness was caused by something other than the fact that you're a person of interest in a murder investigation."

She set the bowl on the side table. "Blanche and I used to be friends..."

Sashay stretched and leapt gracefully from the armchair to my lap. When she headbutted my hand, I gave in, stroking her soft fur and scratching under her chin. She purred contentedly, curling up on my thighs.

"What ended the friendship?"

Grandma Elsie crossed her legs. "This may surprise you, but your mom and Blanche's son, Gideon, were engaged for about a year." She sighed. "My psychic intuition gave me doubts about the marriage. So when your mom visited Karma Moon one day, I told her she'd already met her soulmate—but it wasn't Gideon. She ignored my prediction...at least for a while." She sighed. "Then on her wedding day, your mom left Gideon at the altar and ran off with his best friend—your father."

Well, that was quite the bombshell. No wonder Blanche hated our family. Finding out your son's fiancée ran off with his best friend had to sting. Though, it was pretty romantic in a scandalous soap opera kind of way.

I barely spoke to my parents, except for the occasional email. My grandma was the only family I'd ever need and I was grateful to have her in my life.

"Guess that story had a happy ending for at least two people."

Sashay jumped off my lap and sat next to the cat supply bag, licking her paw.

"It might've reopened old wounds when I was setting up Blanche's grandson, Nathaniel, with Angela. Blanche still blames me for ruining the wedding." Grandma's fingers drummed anxiously on her knee. "She's never forgiven me for the embarrassment it caused their family. And now, seeing me accused of murder and being sent to the clink? I bet she's enjoying every minute of it."

Smiling, I shook my head. "I have to ask, just how many prison movies have you seen?"

We laughed. Yet my giggles quickly faded as my thoughts returned to our predicament.

"Your friend Lucinda came by the store and mentioned that her shop had been broken into, and someone stole a poisonous plant that she grows in her greenhouse. Do you think that whoever poisoned Angela is the same person who robbed the florist shop?"

Grandma Elsie absently rearranged the mismatched teacups on the shelf beside her. "I don't see a connection. What type of plant was it?"

"Tanas Root, I think."

Her hand froze mid-reach for another cup. Her rosy complexion lost a good deal of color. "Oh, my. It's highly toxic and can cause rapid cardiac failure if consumed."

"That's what killed Angela..." I tucked hair behind my ears. "I overheard the police questioning Lucinda about the break-in. She didn't lie to the police, but she does look suspicious."

She shook her head. "I've known Lucinda for decades. The woman even has funerals for the plants that die under her watch. She mourns them like a person. There's no way, she'd ever hurt anyone."

I trusted my grandma's instincts and mentally crossed Lucinda off my suspect list.

Sighing, I sank deeper into the worn sofa cushions. The scent of vanilla and lavender from the aromatherapy candles filled the room, but did little to ease the tension in my shoulders.

Two suspects were definitely lying—my neck-tingling-coldness had confirmed that much, but about what? No idea.

My grandma's cornflower-blue gaze fixed on me with concern. "Danika, sweetie, I can tell something's bothering you."

I winced. "Is it that obvious?"

"Only to someone who's watched you perfect the art of dramatic slouching since you were twelve," she said with a hint of a smile.

My body sagged even further. "It's just frustrating, you know? I have this gift to tell when people are lying about things, like cheating on their diet, but it's useless if they genuinely believe what they're saying."

She reached out, patting my knee. "I know it's not easy, dear. My own gift can be an annoyance sometimes, too."

"Yeah, because helping people find true love is such a terrible burden. Meanwhile, I'm over here collecting trust issues like they're tarot cards—making me suspicious of everyone." I let out a self-deprecating laugh.

And boy, did it ever. I was starting to feel like one of those conspiracy theorists who thinks the government is spying on them through their toaster.

Sashay stretched lazily, letting out a disgruntled chirp as if annoyed by my complaining. Her sharp eyes narrowed at me, judgmental as ever.

"Oh, honey." Grandma Elsie's voice softened. "Your gift just takes time to master."

I turned to face her, noting the worry lines etched around her face. My heart squeezed. My so-called gift had always been more of a mixed blessing—like getting a puppy for Christmas only to discover it has a taste for designer shoes.

Sure, knowing when people were lying came in handy, but the occasional headaches? Not so much.

The truth was, I'd spent years trying to ignore my ability. Moving from job to job, city to city, like a tumbleweed with commitment issues. It was easier that way. No attachments meant no one to lie to me, no painful icepick sensations at the base of my skull when they did.

"I'm trying, Nana. But it's not like I can march up to Sheriff Hall and tell him I know my grandma's innocent because my magical lie detector says so. Pretty sure that would land me in a straitjacket or a government lab."

She laughed, the sound brightening the room. "No, I suppose that wouldn't go over well. Though I'd pay good money to see his face."

Okay, yes, I sounded whiny, but when your special ability was basically being a human polygraph, you might complain, too.

Grandma Elsie adjusted the frilly doily on the arm of the sofa. "Think of it more as...guiding the conversation based on your sensitivity. It's all about asking the right questions and listening to what isn't being said." Her smile faltered.

Was it my imagination, or was there something wistful in her tone?

Maybe I'd been looking at this all wrong. Grandma was right, my power wasn't just a lie detector—it was a truth compass. It didn't give me the whole map, but it could point me in the right direction.

And until Angela's murder, I'd never even considered using my gift for anything meaningful. My pulse quickened at the thought of Grandma Elsie's name being dragged through the mud. What if I didn't figure this out in time? The thought of her being arrested made my stomach churn.

With Grandma Elsie under suspicion...it was time to stop

running from who I was. Weird, for sure. But maybe weird was exactly what this case needed.

"You've already caught someone in a lie, haven't you?" she asked softly.

I sat up, tucking my legs under me. "Yeah, I caught two lies today, but they're not exactly helping me crack the case. Hence the whining."

At my past jobs, occasionally detecting lies had been straightforward. Is this expense report accurate? Did that customer try to return a worn shirt? Does this dress make me look fat? But murder was way above my pay grade.

Her expression turned serious. "All I'm going to say is, your gift is a part of you. Embrace it, learn from it, and it will serve you well. Okay? Feel better now?"

"Yeah." I tugged at a loose thread on my jeans. "Thanks for the pep-talk, Nana."

She smiled back, the worry lines around her eyes softening, and for a moment I saw past the confident matchmaker to the grandmother who was probably just as scared as I was. We sat quietly for several minutes.

Sashay spun in circles chasing her tail, making me snort-laugh. The cute cat could always brighten my mood.

"What should we do about the cat?"

"Give her back to the family," she said.

"Oh." I glanced at the bag of cat stuff and my heart panged.

Sashay sniffed the sack. It fell over and she poked her head inside. She strutted out with a soft mouse in her teeth, carrying the toy over to the armchair and playing with it.

"As I was leaving the police station, I saw Nathaniel Harrington. He must be a suspect, too," Grandma Elsie said.

"Nate won't be one for long. I already checked his alibi, although, the man *is* hiding something. And I've narrowed the suspects down to Katherine Harrington, Cassie Peters, and her boyfriend, Patrick Hoang."

"Sweetheart, maybe you should let the police handle the investigation."

"I can't leave this to them. You've always had my back and clearing your name is the least I can do for you."

The words caught in my throat as I thought about just how much she'd been there for me. Including this morning's big reveal from Ryker that she'd made me co-owner of Karma Moon—something that, apparently, everyone had known but me. While I'd been planning my eventual escape from retail, my grandmother had quietly made me her business partner. The irony wasn't lost on me.

I swept hair over my shoulder and we locked eyes. "So...interesting chat with Ryker today. He seemed surprised that I didn't know about my stake in Karma Moon. When were you gonna tell me?"

Her lips twitched. "As soon as you came to your senses and made Mystique your home, silly. I've been putting your share of the profits into a savings account."

"That's incredibly generous of you, but I can't accept any money I haven't earned on my own. It's too much and I don't deserve it."

She scoffed. "Don't be ridiculous. You're my granddaughter and sole heir. Your father never wanted anything to do with Karma Moon and he has made his own fortune." She smiled. "So, is it too late to share my profound grandmotherly wisdom about embracing your destiny?"

I raised an eyebrow. "Is this where you tell me everything happens for a reason? Because I'm pretty sure that's in the Grandma Handbook, between the cookie recipes and guilt trips." I smiled and stretched my legs out in front of me, trying to shake off the weird feeling that maybe she was right.

That maybe ending up here, right when she needed me most, wasn't just another case of my life going sideways.

I hugged her and leaned back. "I love you, Nana, but managing Karma Moon isn't really my *thing*. But I'll stay long enough to make sure you're cleared as a suspect, and then I plan to leave. I hope you understand."

Sashay pounced on a fuzzy ball and sent it rolling across the floor. Her tail swishing, she chased the small toy into the kitchen.

My grandma nodded with a sly grin. "We'll discuss it again in a few months."

"I'm serious. I know it's not what you want to hear—"

"I'm exhausted, sweetheart." She got to her feet and stretched. "Can we talk about this another time?"

"Sure. Get some rest."

She shuffled into the hallway toward her bedroom. I texted Ryker and Keisha to let them that my grandma was home. They wrote back their relief. My own was short-lived. Prison jokes aside, there was still a killer loose in Mystique.

CHAPTER 13

After a long day of restocking the shop until closing, I went to my room. Sitting on the window-seat, while Sashay dozed on the bed, I noticed a mass of grey fur clung to the comforter. Watching Sashay sleep, my heart expanded. She was just too lovable and sweet.

Pen and notepad in hand, I chewed on the end of the ballpoint. Being more proactive was a must. Going vigilante seemed like the only option to catch the killer and get my grandma off the hook.

Now perhaps you're wondering, Danika's a salesclerk in a new-age shop, not an investigator. And you'd be right. So how come I was acting like a homicide detective?

That's the exact thing I was asking myself.

While I had a list of suspects, I needed proof of foul play, or at least a clue pointing me in the right direction. I had plenty of theories on who might've killed Angela. What I didn't have was any substantial evidence. Not a scrap of proof.

In all the crime fiction I'd read, the best place to start was by examining the scene of the crime, followed by the victim's residence.

First, I jotted down some notes on the pad: *Victim: Angela Hernández, stalker and shoplifter, who tries to seduce her former best friend's boyfriend, and is poisoned by a love potion.*

Suspects: Sofia Hernández, Katherine Harrington, Cassie Peters, Patrick Hoang.

Possible motives: Sofia was not a fan of her stepsister. Katherine considered Angela beneath her family. Cassie and Patrick probably wanted Angela to stop harassing them.

I plucked cat hair off my pants, and Sashay pawed at the air in her sleep. Then I added: *Pick up cat treats and salsa from the market. Don't forget a lint roller!*

My thoughts had wandered off. I was supposed to be detailing suspects, not writing a shopping list. This amateur sleuthing gig was hard work.

I placed the notepad on the window seat and headed to the kitchen. In her bedroom, Grandma was resting comfortably, enjoying her favorite classic sitcom.

Seizing a flashlight from a drawer, I went downstairs and out the back door into the alley. The yellow crime scene tape attached to a trashcan and a drainpipe wilted limply over the pavement. I ducked under the tape and examined the area. A cool breeze lifted the hair off my neck as I pointed the flashlight's beam at the ground looking for clues. Only thing I found was an empty soda can and a wad of gum stuck to my shoe. After ten minutes, I gave up and shambled back inside, leaving the flashlight on the kitchen counter.

In my room, I grabbed my laptop, plopped onto the bed, and disrupted Sashay's nap. She meowed and went back to sleep on my pillow. I searched online for Angela's address by using her full name and the town. Her apartment building, Neighborly Nesters, was listed on the first website that popped up. No wonder the reports of stalkers had increased.

Finding someone's info on the internet only took about twelve seconds. It was kind of scary.

I checked the time on my phone, almost midnight. Closing the laptop, I placed it on the nightstand beside a true crime hardback.

Not wanting to go alone, I texted Keisha. Lucky for me she was doing laundry and watching infomercials. I invited her go with me to search Angela's apartment. She agreed and I knew then that she was best friend material. I would've asked Ryker, but being a lawyer, he probably wasn't down for a little B and E. (That's Breaking and Entering, just in case you didn't know.)

I scampered into the kitchen to grab a few items and stuffed them into my backpack.

Keisha texted me when she arrived and I met her outside. She waited by her green Honda, dressed in a black turtleneck sweater, jeans, and ankle-boots. Keisha had styled her hair in a messy ballerina bun on top of her head. I'd pulled my own hair into a high ponytail and wore a black T-shirt with yoga pants and sneakers.

We got into her car and I set the backpack on the floor by my feet. Keisha started the engine and backed out, then drove down Main Street.

"Thanks for coming with," I said. "I know it's late."

Keisha drove past a dimly lit fire station. Unlike the hustle of urban nightlife in a bigger city, Mystique's streets were serene and unobtrusive.

"I'm a night owl and I want to clear Elsie's name as much as you do," Keisha said.

"You don't have to go inside with me. You can just be the lookout."

Keisha sped through a yellow light at the next intersection. "Okay. What are we searching for, anyway?"

"Any type of clue that might lead us to the killer. Maybe Angela kept a diary."

It would be helpful to find a journal, but highly unlikely. Still, I had hope we'd unearth some overlooked evidence.

She glanced at the backpack. "What's in that?"

"Gloves, flashlight, sandwich baggies. And a couple of snacks in case we do a stakeout. Detective stuff."

She nodded. "You're really getting into this investigative work."

I put Angela's address into the GPS on my phone and it guided our way.

Keisha parked the car on the street in front of a closed corner market two blocks from Angela's apartment. We got out and I slung the straps of the backpack over my shoulder. Keisha and I crept through the neighborhood like two spies in the night. It was as quiet as a library, with streetlights casting shadows along the road. We passed a deserted park, the playground silent, and then a house, the lights from their TV flickering through the blinds.

The apartment complex, Neighborly Nesters, was located in an intermediary area, where the older single-story houses were being rehabbed or torn down.

Once we reached the front of the tan stucco building, I marched ahead, trampling the yellowed lawn, with Keisha trailing behind. My nerves were taut, and I kept expecting a cop or the killer to jump out of the azalea bushes.

The two-story structure was built in a U-shape and surrounded a weed-choked courtyard and an empty swimming pool. Outdoor lights on the exterior shone on several rusty lounge chairs huddled near a rotting wooden picnic table and a grimy barbecue. To the left was a gravel parking area with five cars.

I wasn't sure if Angela's apartment was upstairs or down. "Look for number thirteen," I whispered.

Keisha tugged on my sleeve and pointed at a door on the first-floor blocked off with crime scene tape. This must be Angela's residence. My palms started sweating.

The brass numbers on the door were crooked, the three dangling upside down by one nail. I tried the handle, but it was locked.

Keisha gestured for me to follow her and we exited the courtyard. Sticking close to the side of the building, we tiptoed down a backstreet between the apartment building and a spooky-looking boarded-up house. I took the flashlight out of the backpack and switched it on. The beam bobbed over weeds and brown grass. When we reached what I hoped were Angela's windows, I stopped and handed the light to Keisha. A frosted pane above our heads resembled a bathroom window and might not be locked.

Opening the backpack, I withdrew a pair of yellow dishwashing gloves and tugged them on.

"What are those for? Are you going to wash her dishes?" Keisha asked with a tad of snark.

I rolled my eyes. "They're to keep me from leaving any fingerprints. It's all I had in the house."

"Oh, well, that was smart thinking."

"Give me a lift," I whispered, setting the backpack on the ground.

She crouched and laced her fingers together like a stirrup. I placed a sneaker on her hands and she hoisted me upward to the window. I pushed on the glass to raise it and the window slid open.

Huzzah! It was unlocked. Adrenaline coursed through me and I grinned.

Gripping the ledge, I wedged a leg through the opening

and then the other to shimmy inside. Reaching out with my feet, I felt hard porcelain, the toilet. I stepped on the lid and blinked into the darkness.

Spinning around on the toilet, I poked my head out the window. "Hand me the backpack and flashlight, please."

Keisha handed them to me. "Be careful," she murmured. "I'll text you if anyone comes."

After setting my phone to vibrate mode, I positioned the backpack over my shoulders and turned on the flashlight. I was in a small pink bathroom with a fluffy rug and a shower, the floral curtain sagging on the rod. A lone wastebasket sat near the commode.

Moving as quietly as I could, I ventured from the bathroom into a dark hallway with one open door and an archway. Stale, musty air invaded my nostrils. Yanking up my dishwashing gloves, I stopped in the hall between the bedroom door and the archway dividing the rooms.

The apartment was too silent, not even a ticking clock. A creepiness overcame me at being in the home of someone who was dead. It almost felt like an invasion of privacy. The police had definitely been here already. The place was in shambles and they'd had no qualms searching the premises. I felt sorry for Angela and a little angry at the disrespect they'd shown her home.

I could almost imagine what Angela's apartment had resembled before the police had ransacked it. Angela had a minimal, classic style with rustic furniture in colors of silver, blue, and dark chocolate. A kitschy chandelier was suspended from the ceiling.

Stepping into the bedroom, I assessed the mess. Drawers dangled open. Sheets torn off the bed. Clothes strewn on the carpeted floor, along with a pair of fuzzy cat slippers. Framed photos knocked over. Two canvas paintings slumped crookedly on the walls.

After straightening two photos of Angela with her mom and placing them on the dresser, I peeked inside the closet. Just a sad array of Crocs in every color imaginable paired with what looked like a clearance rack explosion at a discount store—bedazzled sweater vests, elastic-waist pants, and enough polyester cardigans to outfit a convention of librarians. Poor Angela. Even her wardrobe was a crime scene.

As I rifled through her belongings, a nagging thought crept in. What was I really looking for? A neon sign saying the killer was here? I sighed, blowing a strand of pink hair out of my face. I had little hope that I'd find anything the cops hadn't.

Since I uncovered nothing of interest in the bedroom— not even a diary or the stolen voodoo doll—I moved onto the living room-slash-kitchen, which was one big space.

The couch cushions lay at odd angles on the floor and the kitchen cabinets and drawers had been left open. The furniture had the same pastoral style and color scheme as the bedroom. I meandered through the kitchen, running my fingers along the countertops, then opened the fridge. Maybe Angela had left a clue there? I wrinkled my nose at the smell of spoiled milk. *Ugh.* Nothing but moldy leftovers and condiments past their prime.

A trash bag had been overturned and decaying food had spilled onto the dingy linoleum. I sifted through the trash and found a torn piece of paper—a DNA assessment with Angela's name on it. Not sure if it was a clue, I folded the paper and placed it in a baggie, then put it in the backpack.

My phone vibrated with a text. I slipped the cell from my pocket.

Keisha: *Find anything yet? It's cold out here.*

Me: *Not yet. Give me 5 more mins.*

Keisha: *I'll check the street. Hurry!*

There had to be something here. Something the cops missed. Something that would prove Grandma Elsie's innocence. I just had to find it.

With hands on my hips, I surveyed the living room. A floral-print sofa faced a small TV on a rickety stand. Magazines and junk mail were scattered across a coffee table, and several framed photos hung crookedly on the beige walls.

I started with the sofa, lifting each cushion and running my fingers along the seams and crevices. Nothing but crumbs, a few pennies, and what looked like a fossilized Cheeto. Moving to the coffee table, I sorted through the pile of papers, scanning each one for anything suspicious or out of place. Most were just bills and catalogs.

A bookshelf in the corner caught my attention. I ran my finger along the spines—mostly self-help books and romance novels. One title made me pause: *Love Spells for the Desperate Heart*. Flipping through it, I found several dog-eared pages and aggressive highlighting, but not much else.

The photos on the walls showed Angela at various tourist spots, always alone. In each one, she wore that same forced smile that hadn't quite reached her eyes. I even checked under the TV stand and behind the curtains. The room felt like it was mocking me with its mundane secrets.

No smoking gun, no convenient confession letter, not even a shred of suspicious evidence. Just the sad remnants of a lonely life.

My cell buzzed again and I peered at the message.

Keisha: *Someone's coming! Get out!!!*

The doorknob to the front door jiggled. My heart galloped and I broke out in a sweat. I ran back to the bathroom and, in my haste, stuck my foot in the wastebasket.

Shaking it off, tissues and a torn receipt tumbled out. Instinct had me snatching the paper and shoving it into my pocket. I climbed onto the toilet, thrusting the flashlight inside the backpack and zippering it. I tossed the bag outside and heard an "*Ouch!*" and cringed. I might've struck Keisha.

Oh, well. I'd apologize later.

I dove headfirst out the window just as the door opened in the living room. I dropped like a stone. Before she could brace herself, I crashed into Keisha and we both slammed onto the ground with a thud.

We scrambled to our feet and she seized the backpack. I didn't stop to close the window.

Keisha hustled along the alley and I sprinted behind her. We rounded the corner and loped to the car. As soon as Keisha got inside the Honda, she started the engine. I had barely made it onto the passenger-seat when she hit the gas and we surged forward. Flipping a U-turn, she speeded down the street. I fastened my seatbelt and swiveled to peer out the back window. The sheriff's vehicle was parked at the curb of Angela's building.

Whew. We hadn't been caught.

Still wearing the yellow gloves, I yanked the tattered receipt from my pocket. It was a credit card slip for a local B&B, the Sleep Inn, with the last name: *Hernández.* A possible clue! I stuffed the receipt into a baggie. This case was so damn frustrating. The more I learned, the less I knew.

CHAPTER 14

Karma Moon opened at ten o'clock, and since Grandma Elsie had a dentist appointment, Keisha and I worked in the shop in her absence. We dusted and straightened the shelves while ethereal flute music drifted from the store speakers.

Keisha gave me a sideways look. "Last night was...fun."

I nodded. "It was pretty intense. Thanks for going with me."

"When I saw the cop car pull up, I freaked out."

"You did good and saved my butt."

She giggled. "We can't have you and Elsie sharing a jail cell."

"No, we certainly can't have that," I agreed. "And we should keep the break-in to ourselves."

"I won't tell a soul."

We went back to work. Keisha kept smiling and stealing glances at me while she tidied up.

"What?" I finally said.

"So what's the deal with you and the smexy attorney?"

Smexy was a fitting term for the smart and sexy lawyer. I

dropped a coconut oil bath bomb that I'd been restocking. It rolled under the table and I crouched to retrieve it. Setting it in the basket with the others, I licked my lips.

"You mean Ryker?"

Keisha grinned wickedly. "You're on a first name basis. Thought-provoking."

"Shut up." I giggled, then sobered. "We're only friends. He's helping me solve the murder."

"Ryker's taken you to lunch."

"How do you know that?" I asked, then rolled my eyes. "My grandma told you. What a blabbermouth! And for the record, lunch is *not* a date."

"Elsie didn't set you two up?" Her flowy peasant blouse slipped off one shoulder.

"Gads no!" I shook my head. "She knows better than to interfere with my love life."

Keisha's lips puckered. "Hmmm."

"What does that mean?"

She folded a bandana printed with crescent moons. "Nothing."

"Keisha!"

Amusement lit up her eyes. "Your grandma's psychic intuition on love is rarely wrong. Obviously, Angela and Nate Harrington were a bad match. When Elsie mentioned you were moving here—"

"*I'm not.* I only plan to stay long enough to keep my grandma out of jail."

She continued as if I hadn't interrupted. "—Elsie said that she'd found your soulmate."

"Oh?" I bit the inside of my cheek. "And you think it's Ryker? I barely know him. Sure, the man is attractive, clever, and charming, but I'm not staying. So there's no point starting a relationship with someone."

As the words left my mouth, they tasted sour. Ryker was a good guy, and I did like him. Maybe a little more than just *like*. It was nice to be around someone who accepted me for who I was and didn't mock my weird six sense. I'd dated my fair share of jerks and he seemed like a genuinely nice guy, and those were as rare as four-leaf clovers. There was definitely a strong attraction between us, but I was a hot mess and Ryker was someone who had his life together—knew what he wanted, while I hadn't any real clue. I admired him for it.

Keisha added two purple crystals to a wicker basket. "Why are you so anxious to leave Mystique? I don't get it."

My mouth worked, but no sound emerged. Finally I managed to mumble, "I don't feel my life's purpose is living in a tourist town and working in retail, you know?"

"No. I really don't." Keisha regarded me with a mixture of impatience and incredulously. "Living in Mystique gives me and everyone living here a sense of community. Going anywhere isn't a huge hassle because most places are within walking distance, which cuts down on the carbon footprint. And if you ever need help with anything, the residents are always happy to lend a hand. You won't get any of that living in a big city. Plus, retail can be a rewarding and a fun job that pays the bills. Retail isn't easy or beneath anyone."

I glanced about uncomfortably and pushed hair off my face. A hard lump rose in my throat the size of a golf ball. My generous grandmother had offered me ownership in Karma Moon and all I could do was bad mouth her business. I was a bad, bad person.

"I'm sorry if I sound condescending," I said, feeling contrite. "I shouldn't criticize the town or belittle the shop."

For a moment, I considered all of Keisha's reasons. All good ones, if I were being honest. What would it be like to settle here? Give up my nomadic lifestyle? If I stayed here I'd have real friends, stability, and a grandmother that loved me and whom I adored. I would have a real home. It sure would be different and...okay, yes, it sounded pretty awesome.

Yup, that's right. The stubbornly independent Danika Dreary was considering staying in Mystique. What can I say? I was hardheaded.

"I suppose you're right about Mystique, *and* Ryker is swoony." I shrugged. "But there's no point in pursuing a relationship until my grandma is no longer a suspect." I changed the topic. "Are you dating anyone?"

Keisha shook her head and her bottom lip pouted. "Not right now. Your grandma is working on a match for me." She patted my shoulder. "And, Danika, I know your life is going through a rough patch right now, but don't worry, it only lasts through adulthood." She giggled at her own joke.

I smirked. "Comforting."

"I'm going to take a break. I need to return a phone call."

Keisha went into the storeroom while I stayed behind the counter.

Two people entered the shop, and I could tell they were tourists by the way they *oohed* and *aahed* over everything. The man was stout and about an inch shorter than the woman, who was pretty, twentyish, and African-American. Her ruffled silk blouse was a dark maroon and she wore it over jeans and flats. The man scratched his baldhead and shrugged off a cheap sports coat he might have stolen from a used car salesman. He draped it over his forearm, revealing a khaki shirt wet with spots of perspiration around his armpits. His faded jeans were a bit too long, the hem dragging on the floor.

The woman waved at me. "*Yoo-hoo!* Does the tarot reader have any openings today? I want Jack to get a reading."

Jack, the guy she clung to like Velcro, tugged at his sleeves. "I don't believe in that nonsense, Latoya."

"She's at a doctor's appointment. You could come back tomorrow," I said.

Latoya pouted. "What about you? Why can't you do it? *Please*."

"I am too busy right now—"

"It won't take long and the shop's empty," she insisted.

"How about I help you pick out incense or a nice candle instead?" I offered.

But Latoya wasn't budging. "I want Jack to get a reading."

"I'd love to help," I said, forcing a smile, "but like I said, the person who normally does it isn't in today."

Jack stared at me blankly. Latoya stabbed with me a determined squint.

I sighed. Technically, I supposed I could do a reading. I'd watched Grandma Elsie do tarot since I was a toddler. Hmmm...might even be fun. But I would not get sucked into this life. I prided myself on being able to say *no*.

"I'm sorry. This just isn't a good time," I said.

Latoya pulled out a wad of cash from her purse. "I'll pay you double."

"Right this way." I gestured toward the purple curtain with silver stars that concealed the private room.

"Divine!" Latoya clapped.

You can stop sneering. I could say no if I wanted to, but let's face it, I had bills to pay, a cat to support, and my savings could really use some padding.

Pulling back one side of the curtain, I led the couple into the adjoining room. A dark-blue tapestry printed with gold moons and stars lay over a round table with three chairs. The ornate chair with a high-back was the one my grandma used, so I went around the table and claimed it, then gestured at the other two chairs. A single lamp rested on a shelf with a cloth draped over it to mute the light.

The couple sat, and Jack leaned back, crossing his arms. It was obvious he was indulging his, um, girlfriend—wife—friend?

I lit a tea candle and pushed the glass crystal ball resting on a mahogany stand in the middle of the table to one side. "Do you want the twelve or three tarot reading today?"

"Whatever," Jack replied in a bored tone.

"Three-card draw, please." Latoya said.

I picked up the deck on the shelf with the lamp and handed them to Jack. "Shuffle the cards and concentrate on one area of your life that you want an answer to."

After shuffling the cards, he set the stack in front of me. "Hit me."

Latoya giggled and elbowed him. "This isn't twenty-one."

I smirked. "Please take the following guidance with a margarita rim of salt." I flipped over the first card: *The Hanged Man*. A chill goosebumped my skin as I stared at the card. I had the strangest feeling it was meant for *me* instead of him.

"This card represents how you feel about yourself," I said. "You feel bewildered and perhaps fearful because you sense there's something that you need to surrender to be truly happy. This means it's time for a new phase in your life. Maybe you should view things from a different perspective."

Huh. Was this card telling me to give up my goal to move? Or that I needed to change my outlook? I guess working retail wasn't *that* bad. But did I want to stay in Mystique? That was still a big ol' question mark.

I laid the second card face up on the table: *The Sun*. "This one represents what you want most right now. If you're feeling restless, it means you seek contentment and stability in your life." I grasped the third card and set it beside the others: *Judgement.* "This card represents your fears. You're afraid that the objective you've been desiring is being delayed. But don't worry, any choices you make over the next month will only change your life for the better."

Latoya grinned. "Amazing! Thank you. This settles it. We're getting married." She gripped Jack's arm and hauled him up. She withdrew two twenty-dollar bills from her pocket and tossed them on the table. "Keep the change. Let's go, Jack."

Jack nodded in stunned silence. Then he smiled and kissed her cheek. "Okay."

The happy couple left, and I sat there studying the cards. They certainly signified my own thoughts and worries about life. I'd always defended my vagabond existence, and yet it also felt truly lonely at times. Living without a permanent residence or any real responsibilities was a great way to feel empowered and independent. And I was able to do whatever I wanted, but usually alone.

I had to admit, it felt good to help that couple. I placed the cards in the deck and left the room. Near the front of the store, Keisha was helping a lady pick out incense.

Sofía Hernández, aka Miss Odoriferous, traipsed through the front door and proceeded straight toward me. I inwardly groaned and dashed behind the counter to put space between me and her obnoxious perfume. She wore a brightly colored scarf over a yellow sundress and heels. Her mourning period had officially ended—how long had it been? A day or two?

"Nice to see you again, Sofía," I said.

It wasn't nice to see her. It was awkward as a dog wearing roller skates. I'd found her stepsister's body and my grandma was a suspect in her murder. No amount of diet Mountain Dew and tacos could cure the awkwardness I felt.

Sofía flounced up to the counter. "Hi, chica. How you been?"

Her strong floral and vanilla fragrance pummeled my nose and I held back a sneeze. "Good. Great. What about you?"

I bit the inside of my cheek. *Ah, stupid question.*

Sofía sighed dramatically. "Busy. Planning a funeral is time-consuming. And who knew funerals were so expensive? *Ugh.* Angela's dead and they want to celebrate, throw a damn party! Outrageous, right?"

I struggled to breathe through my mouth. "Uh, funerals aren't really a celebration," I said. "More like a way to say goodbye to a loved one. Maybe it's important to them."

"Whatever." Sofía reached into her purse and retrieved an engraved invitation on white card stock. She laid it on the counter between us. "This is the invitation to Angela's funeral. Please give it to your grandma."

I left it on the counter. "That was…fast. How did you get invitations printed so quickly?"

She shrugged. "Angela's biological father is handling everything. I guess he has influence and the money to burn."

"Thank you. I'll make sure my grandma gets it."

"You can come too if you want. *Adiós.*" Sofía flounced out the door.

My first party invite in Mystique was for a funeral I didn't want to attend. Could life get any weirder?

Erm…don't answer that.

CHAPTER 15

I'M HAPPY TO REPORT THAT SEVERAL DAYS HAD PASSED without any more customers dropping dead. Maybe my bad karma was finally turning itself around. I had been working non-stop. Grandma Elsie had been training me on how to handle online purchases and she taught me how to order more stock from various vendors. I think she was just trying to keep me occupied so I'd stay out of the murder case. Not gonna happen. Sure, I had bills to pay, but my next day off was devoted to resuming my investigation.

On an early Saturday morning, Grandma Elsie came into the living room wearing a simple dress, black as old blood, and worn flats. Tears lined her soft blue eyes.

I had been sitting on the sofa and tossing feathery toys at Sashay to chase around the room. When I finally got around to telling the Hernández family that I had Sashay, I'd box up the cat stuff that I bought to send with her. My heart squeezed at the thought of Sashay leaving. But I couldn't get emotionally involved. Right?

"What's wrong? Where are you going?" I asked, straightening.

Grandma Elsie sniffled. "Angela's funeral. The service is being held at the cemetery, Mourning Mortuary, and I'm closing the shop for the day."

I had been so busy lately that I'd forgotten all about it. I'd read in one of my true crime books that killers often visited the funeral of their victim and I wanted to find a new suspect for the police to look into. And I'd bet my last jar of salsa that the killer was going to the funeral today.

"You shouldn't go alone," I said, and meant it. "A funeral means all suspects on deck. This might be a chance to suss out the killer."

"Danika, I really don't think—"

"Give me ten minutes!"

I jumped up and went to my room to change into a black long-sleeved shirt, slacks, and low heels. Then I applied makeup and red lipstick. *Yes*, I was one of those women who didn't like to be seen in public without her face on. My hands shook, but two coats of Great Lash calmed my nerves. Mascara brought out the cobalt-blue in my eyes, and helped me look more awake. I picked the clumps of mascara from my eyelashes, ripping out one or two in the process. Then I blotted my lipstick on a folded tissue, and I was funeral ready.

When I returned, Grandma Elsie reclined on the couch. She stared at the wall lost in thought.

"Nana? You okay?"

She didn't respond. I went to Grandma Elsie and knelt in front of her, placing my hands on her knees. Her head turned in my direction and the sorrow in her gaze made me tear up.

"You don't have to go through this alone. I'm here."

Grandma Elsie patted my hand. "I appreciate that, sweetheart. I called Keisha and she's driving us to the cemetery." Grandma Elsie wobbled to her feet. "She's waiting outside."

"We'll be back soon, Sashay." I waved goodbye to the cat as she pounced on a ball stuffed with catnip.

Grandmas Elsie and I exited the building, and Keisha's green Honda Accord was idling at the curb. Grandma Elsie claimed the passenger-seat and I slid into the back. Keisha was dressed in mourning attire too: an onyx blouse with rayon slacks and kitten heels. Her warm brown skin had a soft glow in the sunlight and her thick mane was styled in a French-twist.

Keisha drove across town, passing several businesses, and I grinned at the clever names: One More Page, a bookstore, Denton Fenders, a car repair, and Murder, She Roach, a pest control. Inside a coffee shop, Brewed Awakening, I spied three elderly ladies sitting near the window sipping from steamy mugs. Tourists meandered along tree-lined streets while browsing in the antique shops. The foliage boasted fall colors in gold, auburn, and red.

"Will there be a wake or reception after the funeral?" Keisha asked.

My grandma shook her head. "No. Just the graveside service."

"Keisha? How well did you know Angela?" I asked.

"We went to high school together, but socialized in different crowds. Angela was best friends with Cassie Parker until graduation." Keisha slowed and veered left, driving through a residential area.

My brows knitted. "The same woman that she was harassing?"

Grandma Elsie grunted. "Angela couldn't understand why Cassie's beau was never interested in her. Although, it was quite simple—he wasn't her intended."

"You sound like a cheesy Harlequin novel," I quipped.

Keisha snickered. "Let's just say, Angela was a modern-day woman who took stalking to a whole new level."

"I remember you mentioning that," I said. "Angela had an unhealthy infatuation with that guy, Patrick."

Keisha glanced at me in the rearview mirror. "Understatement. I overheard Cassie and Patrick arguing about it at the café. Cassie said Angela was leaving nasty notes on her car and writing hurtful comments on her Facebook posts. Angela had her laser focus aimed at Patrick, and if you ask me, he liked the attention."

If this was true, Angela's death could've been a crime of passion or jealousy. It seemed Cassie had a giant burrito of motivation to kill Angela.

"Do you think Cassie or Patrick will be at the funeral?" I asked.

"We're about to find out," Grandma Elsie replied.

Keisha turned into the cemetery, Mourning Mortuary, surrounded by a wrought-iron fence. Large oaks rose majestically among the graves and rolling green lawns. Keisha parked behind a two other cars and one limousine.

Malachi Weatherby waited in the driver's side of the limo, reading a newspaper. His head lifted as if sensing my stare. Weatherby glared at us as if he shared the Harrington family's dislike of any Drearys. The majordomo gave me a serious case of the creeps.

Sheriff Robert T. Hall leaned against his squad car with his arms folded. His gaze narrowed on Grandma Elsie, then me. He nodded in our direction, then returned his attention to the mourners.

The lawn was freshly cut and as green as the felt on a brand-new pool table. Crisp autumn air ruffled the leaves and a family of squirrels scampered up a tree. In the distance, church bells rang out the hour.

The three of us joined the funeral-goers assembled around the casket. Just about everyone here was a suspect. In attendance were Blanche Harrington, and her son Gideon Harrington, along with his children, Nate and Katherine. Mrs. Harrington wore an ankle-length dress, and Gideon appeared regal in a designer suit. Nate waved at me, dropping his hand when he caught Katherine scowling. They were both dressed in dark-blue clothing. When Katherine shifted her weight, her stilettos stabbed the damp grass like sharp blades.

The tension in the air was so thick, you could slice it with a hatchet. The elder Harringtons eyed Grandma Elsie and me as if mentally fitting us for cement waders. The animosity was so intense, it made me feel like a rabbit with its leg trapped in barbed wire.

"Why are the Harringtons here?" Keisha whispered.

"Maria, Angela's mother, has been their housekeeper for over twenty years," Grandma Elsie said.

Keisha leaned close to my ear. "I bet Maria knows all their dirty secrets."

My stomach tightened. What if Angela discovered something about the Harringtons from her mother? Would those secrets be worth killing Angela over?

My grandma's best friend, Lucinda Mayfair, was there, too. She dabbed at her watery eyes with a lacy handkerchief. She wore a fifties-style dress with a flower print pattern and a puffy skirt that seemed inappropriate for a funeral.

"Nana," I whispered. "Why isn't Gideon's wife here?"

Grandma Elsie leaned closer. "Eleanor's rarely seen in public. I hear she suffers from agoraphobia. The only time she goes anywhere is to their beach house in Los Angeles."

A handsome Asian man, wearing dark attire, stood apart from the others. He was about six-foot-two with an angular face and cheekbones a supermodel would kill for. He had nice full lips, black eyes and hair, and a noticeable birthmark on his neck. Tears misted his eyes, and occasionally he wiped at them with a hankie.

I jabbed Keisha in the ribs with my elbow. "Who's that?"

"Patrick Hoang, the object of the late Angela's obsession," she whispered. "But I don't see his girlfriend, Cassie Peters."

If the rumors were true, I couldn't blame Cassie for not liking Angela. Who wants another woman pursuing her man? Patrick's presence seemed odd, though. Why attend the funeral of your alleged stalker?

Your guess is as good as mine.

Angela's stepsister, Sofía, looked quite suave in a dark-purple, knee-length dress. Her makeup appeared flawless—smoky eyes, lots of black liner, and vampy red lips. She stood beside an older Hispanic couple.

Keisha tapped my arm. "That's Luis and Maria Hernández, Sofía and Angela's folks. Your grandma fixed them up. Luis is the local plumber. He was also a widower with a daughter. Maria was a single mother when they met and Luis adopted Angela when she was ten."

A minster hovered near the coffin holding a Bible and behind him was a huge carnation funeral wreath that Lucinda must've provided. After a short eulogy in Angela's honor, the minster recited from the good book, and everyone bowed their heads in prayer.

After the service, we went to pay our respects. Sofía's parents were thanking the minster. The closer we got to Sofía, the heavier and more overpowering her perfume became.

"How are you holding up?" I asked, my eyes watering from the smell.

Sofía sniffled. "I don't understand who could've killed Angela. It's so terrible, I could cry."

A coldness zipped up my spine and chilled my neck. She was straight up lying. But what about? Missing her stepsister? Was she just putting on an act? Yet I felt sorry for her. I didn't know what it was like to lose a sibling, but I did understand loss.

Sofia must've mistaken my teary eyes for heartfelt emotion because she impulsively hugged me, enveloping me in a malodorous cloud. I held my breath and untangled myself from her arms.

"You are so sweet, chica," Sofia said. "You didn't even know my stepsister."

"Please accept my deepest condolences," I mumbled, curbing the impulse to cover my nose. I did manage to step back several feet.

"Angela was a lovely woman and will be greatly missed," Keisha said solemnly and awkwardly patted Sofia's shoulder.

"Seriously? Nobody really liked Angela..." Sofia's voice died away.

Truth. The cold piercing my skin warmed.

"You shouldn't speak ill of the dead," Grandma Elsie chided. "Angela had her issues. She was a fragile woman in need of guidance." My grandma excused herself to talk with Lucinda.

Sofia stared after her, her mouth twisting into an ugly grimace. "Fragile, my fanny," she muttered.

I stared at Sofia, slack-jawed. What an odd thing to say at her sister's funeral.

"Is Angela's dad here?" I asked, examining the mourners. Sheriff Hall had already left. "Does he live close by?"

Sofia shook her head. "Angela never met her father. Her mama would never tell her who he was, but I overheard Maria saying he lives in town and he paid for the funeral."

Hmmm. I recalled the DNA assessment I'd found in

Angela's apartment. She must've been trying to find her father, or she had an inkling who he might be and needed proof.

"Sofía?" I said, tensing up. "I forgot to tell you that I have Sashay, Angela's cat. I found her the night…" A wad of sorrow lodged in my throat. I swallowed. "Anyway, you can come by anytime to pick her up."

Sofía wrinkled her nose. "No thanks. You can drop the flea-ridden thing off at the local shelter."

My head jerked back. I started to protest, then stopped. Keisha and I exchanged shocked glances.

"Maybe your parents want Sashay—"

"They don't have time to care for an animal. *Adiós*." Sofía smoothed the wrinkles from her dress and ran a hand over her tumble of dark hair. She sauntered off to talk with Patrick.

Keisha grunted. "What a coldhearted—"

"No verbal mudslinging," I said. "Not today. Sofía's grieving in her own way."

"Sure, she is," Keisha said with an eye roll. "And that perfume!"

"I know. Someone needs to tell her it's suffocating."

I grabbed Keisha's arm, and traipsed over to Maria Hernández.

I tapped her on the shoulder. "Excuse me."

She turned around. "*Sí?* What do you want?"

Keisha faintly smiled. "Hello, I'm Keisha. I went to school with Angela. I just wanted to give you my condolences, Mrs. Hernández."

The woman nodded, teary eyed. "*Gracias*."

"I'm Danika Dreary, Elsie's granddaughter. I'm so very sorry for your loss," I said, my eyes downcast. "And I wanted to tell you that I have Angela's cat."

The woman stared at me blankly.

"Sashay? A fluffy gray cat..." I said.

Maria's expression dawned with understanding. "*Sí*, yes. I cannot care for the animal. You can have her, yes?"

I nodded, tears lining my eyes. "I'll take really good care of her. I promise."

Maria patted my shoulder. "*Buena*." She scampered off to join her husband and the minster.

My heart felt lighter. I was glad Sashay could stay with me and my grandma now. My eyes filled. Maybe I could even talk Grandma into keeping the cat so when I visited Mystique I could see Sashay.

Oh, stop snickering. *Fine*. I'll admit it. The fluffy gray cat already felt like family.

Sofia and Patrick stood near a towering oak with their heads close together and speaking in hushed voices.

Talking about insurance policies? I doubted it, even though they worked together. I'd trade my favorite Ruby Woo lipstick to find out what those two were whispering about. Sofia started to cry, and Patrick wrapped his arms around her, patting her back soothingly. Over her head, Patrick's fierce stare caught mine, and for a second, I felt like an insect caught in the clutches of a spider. He pulled away and cracked his knuckles.

I averted my gaze. Patrick evidently didn't like me observing them.

"Danika?" Keisha said. "You okay?"

I let out a gusty sigh. "To be honest, I'm feeling out of sorts and I think I put my underwear on backwards."

Keisha smiled at my joke. "I know just how you feel."

"And I'm getting bad vibes from Patrick Hoang."

She nodded. "He's an arrogant jerk. I'm gonna join your grandma. You coming?"

"I'll catch up in a minute."

Keisha joined Lucinda and Grandma Elsie talking to the priest. I wandered the perimeter and paused behind Gideon, Katherine, Nate, and Mrs. Harrington. They didn't see me standing behind them. I pretended to take off my shoe and shake out a pebble.

"I'm surprised Patrick showed his face," Katherine said.

"Weren't Angela and Cassie best friends in high school?" Nate asked, pushing up his round-framed glasses.

"Until Cassie started dating Patrick," Katherine replied. "I guess Patrick won't have to choose between them now."

A love triangle could get wildly out of control. What if Patrick was secretly seeing Angela behind Cassie's back and she found out? Cassie had become my lead suspect. I hoped the sheriff would make an arrest soon, and Grandma Elsie and Nate would be in the clear.

"No gossiping at a funeral. It's undignified," Gideon scolded.

"I am going to express my sympathies to Maria, then we're leaving," Mrs. Harrington said.

Mrs. Harrington and Gideon strolled over to the Hernández family. I stayed put. Eavesdropping could be quite informative once you got the hang of it.

"What did you mean by that remark, sis?" Nate asked.

"Rumor has it, Patrick's been cheating on Cassie with another woman. I bet it was Angela," Katherine said, a dark tone coloring her words. "I hear they've been meeting once a week at that bed and breakfast, Sleep Inn. Maybe Cassie found out and killed her."

This confirmed my hunch even more. Cassie was the killer. *Oh!* I recalled the credit card receipt that I'd found in Angela's apartment for a night at a B&B. Angela must've used her credit card to book a room for her and Patrick.

Nate linked an arm through hers. "How can you be sure?"

"You can learn everything you need to know in this town at the salon. While I was getting a manicure last week, I heard Patrick was seen twice entering the inn with a dark-haired woman. It had to be Angela," she replied. "Just be glad you never dated that psycho."

Nate and Katherine strode to the limousine, where Mrs. Harrington and Gideon waited. Mrs. Harrington caught me staring. She looked at me with disgust as if I was a child who didn't make it to the bathroom on time. Then the pretentious Harringtons piled into the limo and drove off.

I had to know if what I'd overheard was true. Time to have a talk with Patrick. Before I could interrogate him, Sofía appeared at my side. Her perfume stung my nose and I swear it was burning away my nostril hairs, but I sucked it up.

Sofía sniffled. "I don't think Angela's death truly hit me until today, chica."

Her emotions were up and down like a yo-yo. If you're going to pretend to be in mourning at a funeral, particularly one this short, you'd carry it through the whole time, wouldn't you? Sofía's strange behavior was making alarm bells go off in my head. What if...she was the killer?

"I hope they catch whoever did this." I sighed. "There's a rumor about Patrick and Angela secretly hooking up. Do you think it's true?"

Sofía's head snapped back. "That's nonsense! Patrick was appalled by Angela's behavior, the way she was always throwing herself at him. It was disgusting."

"Sofía!" her father called. "Time to go. We're heading out to get ice cream."

"*Adiós*, chica." Sofía shambled off after her parents.

The other mourners were leaving, too. Grandma Elsie stood near her first husband's grave and I joined her. I had adored my grandpa and enjoyed fishing with him on my summer vacations as a child. My grandpa had helped build one of the local churches and even ran the town newspaper, *The Mystique Bulletin,* for thirty years. In his youth, he'd been the author of a bestselling series of crime novels and we'd shared a love of reading. I still missed him.

Grandma Elsie clasped my hand while we paid our respects in reverential silence. When we finished, we met Keisha at the car and drove home.

At least the funeral had been somewhat informative. I'd learned that Patrick had been secretly hooking up with another woman, and I wondered if Cassie knew about the affair. And if that offense was a motive to poison Angela.

CHAPTER 16

The following day, I worked with Grandma Elsie and ignored inquiries by curious patrons about Angela's death. It almost made me cringe at the way the residents had become so invested in small-town hijinks and murder. And don't worry, I forbid Grandma Elsie from accepting any new matchmaking clients until I solved the case.

Midway through the day, during a slow period, I dusted the shelves and mentally started going over my list of suspects, starting with my own personal fave—Cassie Peters. Along with Patrick Hoang, Katherine Harrington, and Sofía Hernández, who were close seconds. Crimes like murder were composed of four parts: motive, means, method, and opportunity. And I was pretty sure that my suspects had all four working against them.

Next up? Questioning Cassie and Patrick.

Sashay entered the main sales floor through the curtains obscuring the storeroom. She carried a crisp leaf in her mouth like a lioness returning to the pride with a fresh kill. Sashay laid it by my foot. Another strange offering from my cat.

Wait, she wasn't *my* cat. I didn't want a pet. Not even this sweet, gift-giving feline. I could not form any attachments while I was here...

Sashay sat beside me, tilted her head upward, and yowled again.

Crouching, I took the leaf, then scratched the cat under the chin. "Thank you."

Sashay purred and rubbed her head against my hand, so of course, I gave her an extra good cheek rubbing. She was so adorable that my heart thawed a little more. I kissed her head and straightened. Sashay moseyed back to the storeroom.

Grandma Elsie ambled over to me. "You have an admirer."

"Sashay's just grateful to have a new home and not end up at the shelter," I said, placing the leaf on the counter.

Grandma Elsie wore a half-smile. "I think it's more than that. You two have a bond."

"You think?" I said and my heart jerked in my chest. "I've always liked cats, but I couldn't have any pets at boarding school or in college. Later, I moved around too much to even consider a pet."

She shrewdly grinned. "Maybe that'll change."

I bit back a smile. She was trying to get me to stay.

Yeah, good luck with that, Granny.

The rest of the day went by quickly and I actually had fun helping people find what they needed, either a gift for a friend, a crystal to speed healing, or a book on interpreting dreams.

Near closing, I wandered about touching the eclectic merchandise and straightening the books. Sunlight streamed through the blinds and lit the shop aglow. The store really was pretty with the shimmery turquoise fabrics hanging from the ceiling and twinkling fairy lights around the windows and counter. A sense of pride warmed my chest and suddenly I felt honored to work in such a wonderful place full of good intentions, love, and compassion. Keisha and Grandma Elsie enjoyed helping people, and I had to admit that it was a truly rewarding feeling to help others.

At five o'clock, Ryker strode into Karma Moon while I was stocking candles and Grandma Elsie was giving someone a tarot reading in her private room. I'd told her about my own tarot experience with that couple and Grandma Elsie had said she was proud of me for taking initiative. I was kind of proud of me, too.

When I saw Ryker, I thought about what Keisha had said about Grandma Elsie claiming Ryker was my...soulmate. But then again, Grandma Elsie had been wrong about Nate and Angela. Maybe she was wrong about this, too. Soulmates? Such malarkey.

I grinned at Ryker and set the last candle in the bin. "Hi."

Ryker smiled, a sexy grin that could melt steel. "Hey, Danika. How are you?"

"Actually, I'm fine. Also, fickle, insecure, a touch neurotic, and indecisive."

Ryker chuckled. I liked a guy who got my sense of humor.

I know what you're thinking, but I could admire a guy without going all swoony. Stop it. I could!

"Sorry I asked," he joked.

I grew serious. As charming as Ryker was, I had no time for romance. I had a murder to solve and a grandma to save from a lengthy stint in prison.

"I want to talk to Cassie Peters and her boyfriend, Patrick," I said. "I've heard from several sources that Angela was after Cassie's man, and she wasn't too happy about it, which makes her my prime suspect."

"What about Patrick? Is he a suspect, too?"

"Definitely." I nodded. "You free tonight? I don't want to question them alone."

He nodded. "Cassie works at the library. It doesn't close until seven. We can go by and see if she'll talk to us, then we can track down Patrick."

"Are you friends with either of them?"

"Not really. Patrick does my insurance so we're friendly," he said.

Grandma Elsie passed us wearing a slight smirk and escorted her client to the door. That old lady thought she was clever with her not so sly matchmaking. But I was onto her sneaky ways and I'd put a stop to it. How you ask? Well, I was open to suggestions.

When they were out of earshot, I spoke. "At the funeral, I overheard Katherine and Nate talking about Patrick meeting a dark-haired woman at a B&B in town. Could Patrick have been cheating on Cassie with Angela?"

Ryker rubbed his chin. "We'll have to find out. I'll close my office and be back in ten minutes." He said goodbye to Grandma Elsie as he left the store.

She locked the door and flipped the open sign to closed. "Do you want to order takeout for dinner?"

"I'd love to, but Ryker is picking me up in a few minutes."

"Another date?" she teased.

I rolled my eyes. "*Nooo*. I have more people to speak to about the case."

Grandma Elsie huffed. "You're not an investigator, Danika. Let the police do their job."

"I'm only helping weed out suspects," I insisted.

Grandma Elsie went around the counter to the cash register. "Is that what you're going to wear?" she asked, counting the money.

I frowned down at my ripped jeans, a striped black-and-white tank-top under a fuchsia cardigan, with my lime-green sneakers. "What's wrong with my outfit? I look casual cute." This morning, I'd styled my long mane into a French braid that hung down my back and showed off my silver hoops.

"At least wear a little fragrance," she said, closing the register drawer.

"We're only friends and Ryker's helping me solve a murder, Nana, remember? No matchmaking," I said in a mock stern tone.

"I would never dream of it, sweetheart."

Did I believe her? Not for a second.

A knock on the store door ended this senseless conversation. I went to the door, unlocked it, and opened it for Ryker. He stepped inside as Grandma Elsie vanished beyond the black drapes.

"Let me grab my purse," I said.

I bustled through the shop, slipping into the storeroom. Grandma Elsie appeared by the staircase, lifted a bottle, and squirted my chest with a blast of peach scented body spray.

"*Ah!* Whaddya do that for?" I exclaimed, coughing as the perfume invaded my sinuses.

She had a twinkle in her eyes. "It was just a spritz."

"Danika?" Ryker called. "Everything all right?"

"I'm not sure, but I smell really good!" I shouted. "Be right there."

Grandma Elsie laughed. "Have fun. And don't wait up for me, I'm playing poker with Lucinda and the girls tonight." She went upstairs with a wry smile.

My grandma had more of a social life than me.

I sniffed my sweater. The fragrance did smell lovely. I grabbed my purse from a shelf and a set of the keys from a wall hook, then met Ryker by the front door. I'd never seen him in casual clothing and thought he looked extra handsome in a V-neck cotton shirt, worn jeans, and soft leather boots. He smelled really good too; the aroma of orange blossoms and cedarwood teasing my senses.

We left the store and I locked up behind us, tossing the keys into my bag.

"Would you like to walk? It's not far to the library," Ryker said.

"Sure, walking sounds good," I replied, falling into step beside him. "Though I should warn you, with my luck lately, we might stumble across another body."

The autumn breeze ruffled my pink hair as we strolled down Main Street. The tourist crowds had thinned out, leaving just a few window shoppers admiring the antique displays and art galleries. I snuck a sidelong glance at Ryker. Even his walking style was put-together—confident strides that made my somewhat slouchy amble look ungainly in comparison.

Ryker's eyes crinkled with amusement. "In that case, I'm glad I specialize in wills and estates. Though I should probably start branching out into criminal law if you're making a habit of this."

We laughed, and I dodged a pile of crispy leaves someone had neatly swept to the curb.

Karma Moon was in the heart of the downtown and we strolled along the tree-lined sidewalk in the clutches of autumn's glory. I was glad we'd decided to walk through town, the air felt crisp yet invigorating. Beyond the buildings were towering trees and lush greenery. I really did love nature and Mystique's charming appeal.

"Is that peach I smell?" Ryker asked, leaning slightly

closer as we walked. "It's nice. Makes a refreshing change from dusty law books and coffee."

"Thanks, counselor," I said, trying to hide my smile. "Though I usually smell more like *eau de* taco truck."

A middle-aged woman in a sweater and jeans, with a curly-haired little girl, stopped and beamed at Ryker. The child wiped her runny nose on the sleeve of her pink dress.

"Hello, Ryker," the woman said. "Thanks again for donating to the animal shelter fund and providing those bags of food. You are a true gem to this community."

"It was my pleasure, Mrs. Poe," he replied. "Let me know if there's anything else I can do."

Mrs. Poe grasped the child's wrist and they scurried past us. Over her shoulder she said, "Welcome to Mystique, Danika. Tell your grandmother I said hello."

My mouth sagged open. I stared at the woman and child walking down the street.

"How did she know who I was?" I muttered.

"Elsie's been telling everyone that you're moving to Mystique, and I think the night before you arrived, it was announced during bingo at church."

Mystique was definitely a tight-knit community. My eyes started to sting. How could I break Nana's heart, you ask? Well, that was getting harder to do...

The more time I spent in Mystique, the more I'd come to realize, it was a melting pot of diverse people from various cultures and backgrounds. And while a bit cliquey, the residents seemed extremely loyal to their own.

I shook my head with a half-smile. "That devious woman is trying to guilt me into staying."

Ryker wore a sly grin. "Is it working?"

I sighed. "Not you, too."

Yet my insides melted a little. Ryker was hinting that he wanted me to stay. Oh, boy. But I was *not* moving here permanently. I had a plan, remember? To move to the city and get another job, which meant leaving Ryker, Grandma Elsie, Sashay, and Keisha behind. I groaned inwardly. Why did my heart pang at the thought of saying goodbye?

Okay, so maybe I was having second thoughts. Stop judging me.

We passed the historic Hotel Mystique and ragtime music seeped through the windows. Ryker and I meandered left onto a side street and crossed over to an impressive three-story brick building with wisteria climbing the sides. An engraved copper plaque beside the stairs read: Amador County Library. We ascended the staircase to the double-doors, and Ryker opened one for me as we slipped inside.

The scent of *eau de* library, old parchment, and stale coffee, filled the air. The interior was impressive with hardwood flooring and outlined with mahogany bookshelves. A circular desk sat in the middle, with two librarians behind the counter, and a second-floor gallery overlooking the ground floor. A dozen armchairs and heavy oak tables were placed about. Large stained-glass windows shed rainbow colors over the furniture and patrons.

"There she is," Ryker whispered and laid his hand on the small of my back.

Ryker and I strode to a bookshelf on the other side of the main area, where a blonde with pale skin and pouty lips was pushing a cart laden with books in the self-help section. Her golden ringlets framed an oval face, and her well-worn dress had a ketchup stain on her left breast. Cassie resembled one of those women who was once the prom queen and a perky cheerleader, but now out in the real world was looking a little haggard around the eyes.

"Cassie Peters?" Ryker asked in a low voice.

She spun around. "Do you need assistance finding a book?"

I shook my head. "I wanted to ask you about your association with Angela Hernández—"

"I have nothing to say to the press. If you'll excuse me." She started to turn away.

"We're not reporters," Ryker said. "We only want to discuss your relationship with Angela."

"Did you not hear me? I have nothing to say." Cassie twirled a strand of hair around her finger.

"*Please*," I coaxed. "Elsie Dreary, my grandma, is a suspect in her murder and I want to clear her name."

Cassie was quiet a moment, then glanced about. "Oh...I see. My shift's over in five minutes. Meet me outside in the parking lot."

Ryker and I left the library and waited at the bottom of the staircase for Cassie.

An elderly lady, with a shock of bluish-white hair, walking a poodle, paused to let the dog sniff a mailbox. "Hello there, Ryker!"

"Hello, Mrs. Wilde," he said. "How are you?"

"Superb." Mrs. Wilde eyed me closely. "I recognize you—you're Danika Dreary, Elsie's granddaughter. I'm Mrs. Wilde, and we're so pleased you're here. Mystique needs more young people to uphold our traditions."

"Nice to meet you," I said.

"I'm in charge of the local book club," the older woman said. "I hope you'll join us one evening. We recently finished reading *A Whole Lot of Cats* by Kitt N. Caboodle."

Joining a book club would be fun...if I was staying. Huh. Have you noticed that everyone in town seemed to be conspiring against me? Was there a town meeting where they all decided to convince me to become a permanent resident? Well, it wouldn't work.

Yeah, yeah, that didn't sound very convincing to me, either.

"Thank you for the invite, Mrs. Wilde," I said. "I'll try to come."

"How rude of me! This is my rescue dog, Mr. Crumpet," Mrs. Wilde said, pointing at her poodle now lifting a leg and peeing on the mailbox.

I shook my head. Why did everyone have to point out that they adopted their dog? Were they worried that people might become suspicious because it didn't look like them?

Mrs. Wilde cast a glance at Ryker, then back to me. A slow grin touched her lips. "And I see you're already making friends. How marvelous."

Neither of us responded. I flushed and Ryker pulled at his collar.

"Have a pleasant evening." Mrs. Wilde tugged on the leash to urge the poodle to move along.

"The people here sure are friendly," I said.

"Everyone loves Elsie, and they know how thrilled she was that you were coming here…for a visit. Or have you changed your mind?" His brown eyes held a spark of hope in them that made my heart go pitter-patter.

I sighed. "I'll admit, the place is growing on me. It's nice that people all know and care about each other here. You don't get that in a city."

Cassie emerged, glancing about nervously. She strode right past us, motioning at us to follow her to a red Toyota Prius parked in the dim corner of the lot.

"Where is she going? Is she worried about being seen with us?" I whispered.

"I'm not sure. Let's find out."

A prickle of unease quivered down my spine. Was Cassie luring us to a dark spot to kill again? I know, I know. We shouldn't follow her, but we did.

Yes, I was willing to risk my life to get to the truth. No rolling your eyes. I never claimed to be the smartest woman in Mystique.

CHAPTER 17

Ryker and I followed Cassie Peters past two parked cars in the library parking lot. The breeze gusted her butterscotch-colored ringlets off her round face, and she wore a jean jacket over a plain dress with practical shoes.

The wisteria climbing the sides of the brick building hugged the walls in a loving embrace. This part of Mystique had treelined walkways and quaint shops. The temperature was mild, and wafts of wild jasmine tinged the air.

Cassie stopped beside a Prius, leaning against the driver's door. "Who are you and what do you want?"

"I'm Danika Dreary and this is my friend Ryker Van Allen," I said. "We wanted to talk to you about Angela."

"So, you what to know about noxious Angela, huh? Why?"

"My grandma is a suspect in Angela's murder, and I'm trying to piece together what happened," I said. "We heard you and Angela were best friends, so we hoped you could share some insight on her."

"It's true, Angela and I were besties in high school until we drifted apart when I left for college." Cassie puckered her lips. "When I returned to Mystique, things were never the same between us."

"Because you started dating Patrick Hoang?" Ryker asked.

Cassie nodded. "Angela was livid and refused to talk to me about it."

"Is that when she started harassing you? Why was she so upset?" I asked.

"Angela had a huge crush on Patrick all through high school, but they never dated," Cassie said, keeping her voice low. "When I came home from college, Patrick asked me out and we've been together ever since."

"And I suppose Angela wasn't too happy about that," Ryker said.

Cassie raised a hand to tug on a curl. "*Ha!* Angela made that obvious every time she saw us together. She left nasty notes on my car and Facebook posts, threatening to curse me with warts if I didn't stop seeing Patrick."

"That must've been awful," I said.

Cassie's shoulders slumped. "I went to the police, but I didn't have any proof that Angela sent the notes. The police examined them, but she left no fingerprints."

A cool breeze rustled through the maple trees lining the parking lot. Moths had started gathering around the tall security lights that flicked on.

"Do you have any that we can look at?" Ryker tapped his chin with a finger.

Cassie shook her head, her curls bouncing. "Sofía told me to throw them out. Her sister was volatile," she said with disgust.

I perked up. "Are you talking about Sofía Hernández?"

"Sofía's my roommate," Cassie said.

"Clearly, you and Patrick are serious since you've been

together so long." Ryker leaned against a car. "Why let Angela get to you?"

Cassie kept fiddling with her curls. "Yeah, but we have our issues, like every couple."

"And maybe Angela saw the cracks and took that as an opportunity to try and break you two up." I kicked a pebble across the parking lot.

Cassie's gaze wandered to the darkening sky. "Possibly. It didn't help that Patrick refused to confront Angela about her psycho ways. It's like he thrives on female attention, ya know?" Her fingers clenched into fists. "I warned him that Angela wouldn't stop until we broke up or she was dead. I know this sounds awful, but I'm glad Angela's gone. She made everyone's life miserable, even Sofía's."

Huh. Cassie hadn't lied once. I know what you're thinking —maybe she was just really good at faking it with all that hair twirling. But my weird little gift was simple: if someone believed what they were saying, no tingle. If they lie, instant skin freeze.

Ryker's eyebrows shot up. "What did she do to Sofía?"

Cassie tugged on a ringlet, and I worried she'd rip out a clump of hair. "For one thing, their parents doted on Angela like she farted sunshine and rainbows. Sofía's always been in her shadow, while Angela got all the attention. It must've sucked."

I nodded. "Sibling rivalry can get ugly. But murderous ugly?"

Cassie shrugged. "Who knows? Not that I'm saying Sofía did anything."

Ryker folded his arms. "Is Patrick meeting you here?"

Cassie shook her head. "No. He's out of town at an insurance conference in Sutter Creek."

A man carrying a stack of books got into his car and pulled out of the library parking lot.

"Do you know where Sofía was the night Angela died?" Ryker asked.

"Yeah, she was home with me watching TV. Neither of us could've murdered Angela," Cassie replied.

An iciness slapped my nape like a cold hand, setting off alarm bells. *Liar!*

Cassie withdrew a set of car keys from her jacket pocket. She clicked the remote with her thumb to unlock the Prius. An object snagged my attention on the backseat. Looking more closely, it was a voodoo doll made of soft tan fabric. Dark hairs were sewn into the head. Beside the doll was a note written in red pen: *You will pay for what you've done!*

I sucked in a breath. "Where did you get that?" I pointed at the backseat. "A voodoo doll like that was stolen from Karma Moon."

"What doll?" Cassie peered through the car window. "That's not mine. Someone must've put it there."

Ryker stared at the creepy cloth-sewn doll. Cassie went to open the door, but I grasped her wrist to stop her.

"Don't touch the car or the doll. It could be evidence," I said.

"I'll call the police." Ryker whipped out his cell from a pocket and called the sheriff.

"If you didn't take the voodoo doll, then someone is trying to frame you," I said. "Or hex you."

"This isn't even my car! It's Patrick's. I borrowed it while he's out of town because mine's in the shop getting new tires." Cassie's bottom lip trembled. "What do you mean by hex?"

Sheesh, Cassie looked about ready to faint. I almost felt bad for her. Almost.

"Like a curse," I said. "A nefarious one meant to do harm."

"Danika, look again. Cassie has blonde hair and those are black strands stitched into the doll's head," Ryker said. "What if the doll was meant for someone else? Like Patrick?"

Leave it to Mr. Lawyer Man to spot the crucial detail I'd missed.

"The police can analyze the hair and see who it belongs to," I said, then narrowed my eyes at Cassie. "Maybe it's Angela's and you wanted to hex her."

Was I jumping to conclusions here? Maybe. Hey, in my defense, voodoo dolls weren't exactly standard library equipment. Then again, neither were tacos, and I'd give my left flip-flop for one right now.

"I swear it's not mine!" Cassie shivered and wrapped both arms around herself.

No icy neck tingles. Cassie told the truth about the doll. But something about this whole situation felt as off as socks with sandals. And trust me, I'd seen some questionable fashion choices at Karma Moon.

While we waited for the cops, I eyed Cassie more closely and thought over what she'd told us about Angela. Had Cassie gotten fed up with Angela's craziness and took matters into her own hands? Had she wanted to hex Angela with the doll? Then decided to poison her instead?

Sheriff Hall arrived at the library within ten minutes. He must've been close by when he got the dispatch. He confiscated the voodoo doll from Cassie's car with gloves and stuffed it in a plastic bag. He pulled Cassie to the other side of the car to speak to her in private.

Ryker touched my elbow. He lowered his voice and murmured in my ear, his minty breath tickling my neck. "Since Patrick's out of town and I don't have his cell number, we can't speak with him yet, but don't interrogate him without me."

"I won't," I whispered. "I like having you watch my back."

He grinned, peered around me to take a peek at my derriere, and straightened. "It's an extremely nice tush."

I giggled and elbowed him in the ribs. "Are you flirting with me? I hope that wasn't your best pickup line."

"Oh, I've got moves you've never seen."

I smiled. "Holy habanero sauce! Are you quoting *My Best Friend's Wedding*? I love that movie."

He wiggled his eyebrows. "I'm a complex fellow."

"That you are and apparently not ashamed to admit that you like rom-coms. I think I like you even more."

"You like me?" His lips curved into a smile. "This is a convo I definitely plan to continue at a later date."

We shared a smile and my heart thumped.

Sheriff Hall told Cassie she had to come down to the station for more questioning and he was impounding Patrick's car as evidence. Cassie sullenly got into the police car.

Sheriff Hall shut the car door and turned to us. "Danika, may I have a word?"

"Um, sure," I said.

The sheriff trudged around the car to the driver's side and I followed.

"Are you and Mr. Van Allen interfering with a police investigation?" Sheriff Hall asked, folding both arms over his chest.

"No, sir." A flush coursed up my neck. "I'm only trying to...help..."

My sleuthing had put me smack on the sheriff's radar. Again. A place I'd rather not be.

He narrowed his eyes. "You found a body and a voodoo doll. Maybe I should take you along for the ride."

My body jolted like a bolt of lightning had shot through me. I couldn't get arrested. And prison orange was *not* my color. Especially, with my pink hair.

I swallowed. "These were both odd coincidences. Honest."

"I don't need or want your help." The sheriff spoke slowly in case I had trouble understanding him. "You and your boyfriend are not to get involved in this investigation. You hear me?"

"Ryker's not my boyfriend—"

"Did you hear what I said? Or will a night in jail fix your hearing?"

"I understand. I-I'll stay out of it," I lied, heat warming my cheeks.

Seeming satisfied, the sheriff hopped into the police cruiser and drove away. I returned to Ryker.

"What did Sheriff Hall say to you?" he asked.

I sighed. "Just told me to stop investigating, which I can't do."

"You were touching your neck earlier. Was Cassie lying to us about her alibi?"

"Absolutely."

CHAPTER 18

On Saturday after closing the shop at four o'clock in the afternoon, Grandma Elsie invited me to go to bingo with her at the Soul Patch Chapel, but I declined. I just wanted to take a nap and cuddle with Sashay for a while.

When she got home two hours later, Grandma Elsie found me on the sofa reading a cozy mystery on my Kindle, with Sashay on my lap. Since Grandma Elsie was still out playing poker when I got home last night, I hadn't had a chance to tell her anything until now.

"Did you have a nice nap?" she asked, dropping onto the armchair.

"I did, thanks." Sitting up, I told Grandma Elsie about talking with Cassie, the voodoo doll in Patrick's car, and Cassie being hauled to the police station.

"It's not Cassie," Grandma Elsie said through puckered lips. "A woman in love doesn't hex her boyfriend."

I believed and trusted Grandma Elsie's instincts, but not so much on Cassie or Patrick's innocence.

"A scorned woman would hex another woman, though," I said, scratching my cheek. "You know what? A fresh perspective might help shed some light on this investigation." I sat up and set my eReader on the couch. Sashay yawned and hopped off my lap. "I'm going to invite Keisha, Ryker, and Nate Harrington over for dinner."

My grandma tapped her foot. "Danika, while I appreciate you wanting to help find the murderer, I wish you would let the police do their job."

"I'm only speeding things along." I tapped a finger on my chin. "It's too bad we don't have a free-standing chalkboard."

"Whatever for?"

"To help solve this case...hmmm, I need an investigation board, like the police use."

"There's a large piece of white cardboard in the storeroom, and a computer linked to a printer that Keisha uses for inventory and online orders. You can download any images and maps that you'll need," she said.

"Okay, thanks," I said, getting oddly excited. I went into the kitchen to check the fridge's contents. "Do we have everything we need to make tacos?"

"We should." Grandma Elsie followed me into the kitchen.

Sashay tagged along and went to the empty food bowl. She batted at it and meowed. Taking the bag from under the sink, I poured food for the cat. Sashay purred as a thank you and munched on her meal. After putting the bag away, I leaned a hip against the counter. I couldn't take Sashay with me when I left. I moved around too much to worry about having a pet to take care of, but I didn't want her to end up at the shelter, either.

"When I leave, will you take care of Sashay?"

Grandma Elsie gazed at the gray cat. "We'll see."

"What does that mean?" I asked, alarmed. "You can't take Sashay to a shelter or abandon her. This is her home now!"

My grandma shrugged in silence, watching me.

My heart ached. I rubbed my chest with one hand. "Why are you looking at me like that?"

She blinked. "You've grown exceedingly attached to that cat."

Sashay looked up from her bowl with an expression that I interpreted as gratitude and...love. I sighed and smiled.

Grandma Elsie shook her head. "It's fine if you invite your friends over, but just don't tell me you're starting one of those ghastly murder clubs."

"No, but joining the local book club might be fun."

Wait, what? Did I just say that? Joining a book club? In Mystique? Ugh. Talk about getting too comfortable. Because I was still planning my grand escape from this quirky little town...wasn't I?

Taco 'bout a plot twist. Maybe solving this case was messing with my head more than I thought. Or maybe...

No. Nope. Not going there. This was temporary. Just a pitstop on my journey to...somewhere else. Anywhere else.

Grandma Elsie patted my arm. "I think I'll skip your crime meeting. I prefer to stay in my room and read. I don't really have the stomach to discuss Angela's murder, sweetheart."

"No worries, Nana." I hugged her and stepped back.

Grabbing my phone off the table, I texted Keisha, and Ryker, and asked him to bring Nate, and invited them all for dinner. Everyone replied that they'd be over within an hour.

Out the two small kitchen windows, the day was overcast and gray. I put my phone down and wrapped a yellow apron around my waist, then started cooking ground beef in a large skillet. Grandma Elsie helped me prepare the meal: rice, fried tortillas, black beans, and homemade salsa.

Once I finished preparing the dinner, Grandma Elsie

carried a plate to her room, where she had a chair, TV tray, and a small flat-screen television.

I went to the bathroom to reapply my lipstick before going to the storeroom to set up my investigation board. My hope was to narrow down my suspect list. I used a large piece of white cardboard and grabbed a handful of red yarn to link everyone involved together. Utilizing the computer and printer, I went to Google maps and printed out images of the alley—the scene of the crime. Next, I logged into Facebook to get photos of the possible suspects: Cassie Peters, Patrick Hoang, Sofía Hernández, and Katherine Harrington.

Hmmm. I wasn't sure how Nate would feel about my suspicions regarding his sister, Katherine, but he might have insight to share if he remained open-minded. My hope was to narrow down my suspect list.

After everything was printed, I attached the images to the board with a glue stick, then schlepped it and the yarn upstairs. I removed a painting from the living room wall and pinned my board up with tacks. Taking the red yarn, I linked the places and people. In the middle, I drew a red circle with a pen from the kitchen and wrote Angela's name in it. I finished by adding the suspect names under each image.

I'd told everybody to text me when they got here, and my phone started chiming when they arrived. I inwardly cringed at the board and hoped my friends didn't think I was being too morbid or obsessive.

In the living room, Sashay was snoozing on the armchair. I scooped up the cat and my eReader, carrying them into the bedroom, and set both down on the bed.

"Nap in here and we'll hang out later, Sashay." I kissed her head and shut the door behind me.

I went downstairs and through the storeroom to the back

door. Everyone was waiting outside, and I told them that I appreciated them coming and to meet me upstairs.

Nate's brown hair was neatly combed, the part sharp as a razor. He wore ironed preppy attire and Italian shoes. Keisha appeared as fashionable as ever in a lavender blouse, designer jeans, and wedge heels. She gave me a quick hug and went up the spiral staircase.

"Nate," I said, "Can I talk to you for a sec?"

He nodded and pushed up his round-framed glasses. "Sure."

Ryker patted my shoulder as he passed, and the aroma of fresh laundry combined with the masculine scent of black walnut and cedar shampoo made me swoon a little. He wore an onyx T-shirt with darkwash jeans. I liked a man with a sense of style. I couldn't stop myself from observing him walk away and think how nice his butt looked in those jeans. I caught Nate's gaze lingering on Ryker like a happy puppy being reunited with his owner.

"What's up?" Nate asked.

"While I was at the Heartburn Café verifying your alibi, I met a nice guy named James. He wanted to know if you were single."

Nate smiled. "He did? Really? Was he that cute redhead?"

"That'd be the one." I lowered my voice, although we were alone. "So...you're gay."

Nate blushed, his skin turning as red as a traffic light. Fidgeting with his shirt hem, his front teeth clicked. "How? Uh, why do you say that?"

I grinned with what I hoped was an encouraging smile. "It's none of my business, but you can trust me, Nate."

He gnawed at his lower lip. Nate smelled like deodorant, minty toothpaste and old parchment. "Um, yeah, I'm gay.

Man, it feels so good to tell someone. Except no one else knows. I mean *nobody*."

I glanced upstairs. "Not even Ryker? He's your best friend."

The flush spread to his neck. "I know, it's only…"

It dawned on me the way Nate had looked at Ryker.

"You're crushing on Ryker. That's why you lied."

Nate nodded. "But he's seriously straight."

I patted his shoulder. "Well, there's a hot waiter who'd love to take you out."

Nate was silent for several seconds, then cleared his throat. "My family will freak if they find out. They're unbelievably conservative. Please don't tell anyone my secret."

I held a hand over my heart. "It's not mine to share."

Nate and I shared a warm smile, and went upstairs. Nate hadn't cared about being snubbed by Angela, nor was Nate the killer. He'd only lied to hide his sexual orientation from others until he was ready.

We met up in the kitchen and everybody dug into the food I'd set up buffet style on the counter. They claimed the dinner delicious and Ryker had a second helping.

"What's the occasion?" Keisha asked, polishing off a glass of lemonade. "Why did you invite us here?"

"Glad you asked," I said, starting to put the food away. "I wanted to get everyone's opinions on a few aspects pertaining to Angela's case. I know everybody cares about my grandma and knows she didn't kill Angela."

Grandma Elsie entered the kitchen and greeted our guests. "Danika, I'll finish cleaning up. You can go visit in the living room."

"Thanks, Nana."

Everyone gathered in the adjoining room and my guests gaped at the board on the wall.

Keisha walked up to it. "What's this, Danika? A murder board?"

I flushed. "I made it earlier to determine what really happened to Angela."

Nate and Keisha sat on the sofa, and Ryker claimed the armchair.

I gestured to my investigation board. "I've marked locations, glued photos of the suspects, and used the yarn to link everything. I wanted your help fitting the pieces together."

Ryker stood and nodded. "You put a lot of thought into this." He faced the others. "What do we know so far?"

Keisha raised her hand, and Ryker pointed at her. She lowered it onto her lap. "Angela was supposedly stalking Patrick and harassing Cassie."

"Ryker and I talked to Cassie," I said. "She said she was home with Sofía the night Angela died."

"That gives Sofía an alibi, too," Keisha said.

"But Cassie was lying," I replied.

Nate's expression was unreadable. His challenging stare met mine. "May I ask, why my sister is on the board?"

I shifted my weight. "Katherine made it evident that she didn't want you dating Angela and even remarked that she would've bribed her not to date you."

Silence shrouded the room like a heavy wool blanket.

After a few minutes, Nate crossed his legs, one argyle sock poking out from beneath his pants. "Let me see if I understand this, you think my sister is capable of murder?"

"These are only speculations and theories," I explained.

Nate pushed his glasses up the bridge of his nose. "When I spoke to you both at the house, I didn't mean to incriminate my sister."

"You didn't, Nate," Ryker replied, then softened his tone. "Katherine somewhat implicated herself when Danika and I were having dinner the other night, but in her defense, I don't think she did this."

Nate nodded slowly, then blurted, "Are you two dating?"

My face burned and Ryker tugged at his collar. Keisha's face lit up with curiosity.

"We're only friends," I said firmly.

From the corner of my eye, I saw Ryker's mouth turn downward. Was he disappointed? Hurt? Miffed? I wasn't sure.

"Katherine said she'd be willing to bribe Angela to keep her from dating you," I said to Nate. "But I agree with Ryker, I don't feel that's a strong enough motive for murder."

"My sister's a snob to be sure, but killing a woman so she won't date me seems a tad extreme," Nate said. "Plus, Katherine runs a lucrative perfume company and likes to keep her reputation squeaky clean. She'd never risk a scandal like this."

"I agree, so if we can verify her alibi, she'll be cleared as a suspect," Ryker said.

"Now onto Patrick," I said, changing the subject. "Gossip implies he was cheating on Cassie. Maybe it was with Angela and he killed her to keep her from exposing the truth."

"That makes sense," Keisha said. "But I think it was Cassie who really hated Angela and she probably got sick of her interfering in their lives. So one day she snaps and poisons Angela."

"That does seem more probable," I said, then looked at Ryker. "Thoughts?"

"I agree with Nate that it's highly doubtful his family was involved," Ryker said. "Out of everyone on this board, Cassie or Patrick seem to be the most likely culprits."

"What about Sofía?" Nate said. "Why is she a suspect?"

I glanced at Sofía's photo on the board. "Jealousy. Sibling

rivalry. Angela got all their parent's attention and she clearly didn't like her stepsister."

"Not much of a motive to murder a family member," Nate said. "I don't know Sofia very well, but she comes across as more narcissistic, than murderous. I don't think it's her."

"I say we vote," Keisha said, lifting her hand. "All in favor of Cassie as the killer raise your hand."

Keisha and Nate raised their arms, and I did, too.

Ryker sighed. "Put your hands down. Danika and I will talk with Patrick and get his version of the story before we concoct any wild assumptions."

"Anyway!" I said animatedly, pacing in front of the board. Ryker moved out of the way to perch on the arm of the sofa. "At the funeral, I overheard Katherine telling Nate that Patrick was meeting up with a woman at a bed-and-breakfast."

"That's right, she did," Nate confirmed.

"I think Katherine should share that information with the police," I said and glanced at Nate. "Do you think you can convince her to do that?"

He shrugged. "I'll do my best." Nate caught Ryker's eye. "I need to go and you're my ride. I have to work tonight."

Keisha smirked. "I thought you were an unemployed trust fund brat."

Nate chuckled. "Is that really how people perceive me? Well, I hate to blemish my image, but I have a job. I restore rare books for collectors, and I have one arriving today that needs immediate attention." He turned to me. "I want to invite you over for dinner at the manor."

"Me?" I pointed at myself. "That's very nice, but unnecessary—"

"I think it will be a good idea to get to know my family better."

"Your grandmother is not a fan," I said. "I'm not sure I'll be welcome."

Nate stood and touched my shoulder. "Let me deal with her. Please say you'll come."

"All right, then. I'd love to," I said.

Ryker and Nate said their goodbyes and left.

I took the board down and blew out a breath. "I'm no closer to exposing the killer than when I started."

"True, but you're being exceedingly proactive." Keisha shifted, tucking a slender leg under her butt. She was quiet a moment. "Danika, I admire what you're doing, but it could be dangerous. There's still a killer out there and they're not going to be thrilled with you getting all up in their business."

"I'll be careful. You wanna hang out and watch a movie? We could make hot cocoa. I need to get my mind off murderers for a while."

"Sure," Keisha said. "I'd love that."

I grinned. "Go get my grandma while I sign into Amazon Prime."

Something was definitely fishy about Angela's death, and everyone here today suspected Cassie or Patrick. I was inclined to agree with them.

A glare from a streetlight coming through the big bay window, which provided a majestic vista of the forest bordering the town and the street below, shone on the TV. I went to the blinds, and looking out, I spotted someone outside.

Across the street, a man stood on the sidewalk staring up at the second-floor of the building. It was Gideon Harrington, Nate's father. For a minute, I forgot how to breathe. Had he been spying on me?

I stomped downstairs and out the alley door.

CHAPTER 19

When I emerged from the alley, Gideon Harrington faced me. He didn't flinch at my scowl or scurry away. He wore a charcoal three-piece suit with shiny wingtip shoes. His gold cufflinks winked in a patch of light from the streetlamp. Two cars drove past before I could run across the street. Gideon waited, a daunting presence.

The sun was setting over the hillside, a blaze of orange and red hues.

A mint-green town car was parked at the curb a block away. Gideon's watchdog, Malachi Weatherby, waited behind the steering wheel. He wore an espresso-brown suit and his salt-and-pepper hair was slicked back. Weatherby scratched the gray beard covering most of his face as he stared at me through the windshield. He had an grouchy look on his face, the kind you get from missing a meal or two.

Out of breath, I confronted Gideon. "What're you doing here?"

"Danika Dreary." The man held my stare. He was even more intimidating close up. "You're one of those nosey busybodies, aren't you? What have you gotten my son involved in?" he demanded.

His tone was menacing. I took a calming breath, willing myself to stay composed. Except, his accusing glare made my hackles rise.

I threw my hands up. "Nate's helping me solve the case."

A man in sweatpants pushing a French Bulldog in a stroller moseyed past us. We shifted closer to the street.

"Are you talking about Angela Hernández's murder?" Gideon huffed, looking like he wanted to push me off the curb into oncoming traffic. "You should mind your own business before a pretty woman like you gets herself into serious trouble."

Well, that escalated quickly. Was I supposed to be scared? My pulse skittered. Maybe a little.

I felt a hot flush run up my face. "Is that threat?" I asked, my armpits growing damp.

"Just leave my family out of whatever you're up to," Gideon said, his voice dripping malice. "Do you know what happens when you interfere with an ongoing murder investigation?"

I swallowed hard. "Let me guess…the case gets solved?"

"Keep that sense of humor. You're going to need it."

His obvious dislike of me was unwarranted. I wasn't pressuring Nate into helping me, nor anyone else. Gideon's repugnance was clearly from the old wound between our families.

I folded my arms over my chest. "I know why you don't like me or my family. And I'm sorry if my mom hurt you."

Gideon grew dangerously still and glowered down at me. "*Hurt?* Your mother stood me up on our wedding day and ran off with the best man," he said, with all the charm of an aggressive pit-bull.

He made my blood pressure rise. "That has nothing to do

with me or my grandma," I said, taking a step back from the curb in case he decided to toss me in front of a bus.

Several seconds of uncomfortable silence passed. A truck grumbled past, sputtering and backfiring.

"You look like your mother," Gideon mumbled.

I fought a smile at his compliment. I liked being compared to my mother, who had been a great beauty in her youth.

Gideon ran a hand over his face. "Where were *you* the night Angela died?"

He was all business again. I guess the flattery had ended.

"Staying the night at my grandma's apartment above the shop. The next morning, I saw the body in the alley. I didn't even know Angela and I had no reason to kill her. Why do you care?"

Gideon gripped his lapels and puffed out his chest like a rooster. "I plan to run for mayor of this town and I've promised to keep the city streets safe."

A faint tingle of coldness stroked my nape. He was being honest, but also not telling the whole truth.

"I met Angela once, the night before she died," I said. "She seemed like an unbalanced person, but she cared about my grandma. Who, for the record, had *nothing* to do with her murder. Elsie Dreary is a matchmaker, *not* a killer."

Gideon closed his eyes, as if mentally counting to ten. "What time did you find Angela?"

"Does it matter? She'd been dead for a while."

He opened his eyes. "There was no one else with her?"

Starting to get a little irritated with all the questions, I blew out a breath. "Like whom? The person that poisoned her? *No.*" Then I remembered Sashay. "Well, her cat was peeing in the planter box."

"Angela died...alone?" Gideon asked, a flicker of emotion in his voice.

"I guess so," I said softly. "Angela must have been desperate enough to come to my grandma for help. Too bad she never got the chance." A slithery sense of foreboding struck my nerves. "Are you going to tell me why you're asking all these questions?"

A muscle in his jaw ticked. "According to my sources, Angela came by to see Elsie Dreary the night before she died, do you know why?"

Sofía Hernández had asked the same thing when she came into Karma Moon. Why was everyone so curious about it? All I knew was that Grandma Elsie had given Angela a tarot reading and offered some advice on her love life, which Angela ignored. But maybe they were wondering if Angela had told my grandma something—something they didn't want anyone to know.

I stared at him in dismay. "Oh, good grief! Angela was infatuated with a guy named Patrick Hoang, who has a girlfriend. Angela was supposed to go on a date with Nate, but she never showed up. That's all I know."

"I hope you're being honest with me, for your sake."

Well, snap. Another thinly veiled threat.

"I swear on my favorite taco stand that I'm telling the truth," I croaked. My throat suddenly felt like it was coated with dust. "I've heard that several people in town had a serious grudge against Angela, so go interrogate one of them."

"I'll keep that in mind, Danika." Gideon studied me for a long moment, then heaved a sigh. "I have an appointment." The arrogant man spun on his heel and strode away.

My hands balled into fists. What a colossal schmuck. He only cared about what my mom did to him a million years ago and not bringing a killer to justice. I was lucky this guy wasn't my father. I felt sorry for Nate and Katherine.

Gideon was working awfully hard to get me to drop the murder investigation. And call me crazy, but what if he knew Katherine was involved and he was protecting his precious daughter? Or maybe Angela had crossed paths with Katherine and pushed her expensive designer buttons a bit too far.

Although, Katherine was still a suspect, my money was on Cassie. She had motive, opportunity, and means. Anyone could've stolen the Tanas Root from Lucinda's greenhouse. Angela might've pilfered the voodoo doll and love potion, but someone had spiked the tonic. All clues pointed to Cassie Peters. And Hell had no fury like a woman scorned.

Gideon got into the town car, and Weatherby started the engine. As they drove off, I kicked at a pebble, sending the rock hurtling into the street. I'd be damned if I was going to let Gideon intimidate me.

I stamped back inside Karma Moon and spent the evening binge-watching movies with my grandma and Keisha. Outside, the wind started howling and clawing at the shutters. If I were superstitious, which I wasn't, I'd say the shrieking winds were a bad omen and I should get into my Mini-Cooper and hightail it outta town. Except I didn't scare that easily.

CHAPTER 20

On Sundays Karma Moon was closed, and I looked forward to having a day off. Grandma Elsie went to church while I stayed behind to cuddle up with Sashay on the sofa with a crime book on women who kill their spouses.

My phone pinged with a text from Ryker and my traitorous heart did a little flip.

Ryker: *Hey, Danika. You busy?*

I grinned and messaged back.

Me: *Depends.*

Ryker: *On what?*

Me: *Are tacos involved? Or circus monkeys?*

Ryker: *LOL Not that I'm aware of.*

Me: *OK. So really…no tacos?*

Ryker: *Don't you have leftovers to eat?*

Me: *That was breakfast and now it's almost lunchtime.*

Ryker: *Do you want to hang out or not?*

I smiled wider, my thumbs flying over the little keyboard.

Me: *Pick me up in an hour. We need to do more sleuthing.*

Ryker: *Did you know that you are exceptionally distracting?*

Me: *Distracting how? Is it my charisma? Pretty pink hair? Sparkling wit?*

I waited. He didn't respond for a full minute.

Ryker: *The whole package.*

My stupid grin widened. He liked me.

Me: *You are quite the charmer...*

Ryker: *See you soon, Danika.*

Scrambling to my feet, I left Sashay on the sofa and went to my room. I threw off my PJs, showered, and tugged on a pair of cropped jeans rolled at the ankle with a pink Henley tank top, then I layered it with an oversized boyfriend-*esque* cardigan sweater, and slipped into sneakers. Now for cosmetics. Wearing makeup made me feel confident, and it wasn't for anyone else, except me. I applied my makeup, then swiped on red lipstick—now I was date-worthy.

Er, I meant ready for another day of crime solving.

Sashay pranced into the room, jumped onto the bed, and meowed, as if to say, '*Why are you leaving me?*' I felt my heart soften even more.

"I'll be back soon. Take a nap, eat your kibble, and play with your cat toys." I scratched behind her ears and she purred. "We'll have cuddle time when I return. I promise."

She plopped down near my pillow and curled up to nap.

Grabbing my keys, phone, and debit card, I shoved them into my pocket and went downstairs. I strode out the back door into the crisp fall air and my mood lifted. Dry leaves crinkled beneath my shoes and a whiff of smoke spiraled from a nearby chimney. I'd always thought autumn was the most beautiful season of the year. Fall was all about new beginnings. The season changing, the weather. Transformation was all around me and it felt delightfully intoxicating.

Ryker waited on the sidewalk, looking extra yummy in an

ebony wool peacoat over a white button-up shirt, jeans, and leather sneakers. I beamed at him, big and bright.

A faint grin appeared on Ryker's handsome face. "You ready to do more investigative work?"

"Always." I tucked hair behind both ears. "At the funeral, I overheard that Patrick was cheating on Cassie with Angela. They were meeting at the Sleep Inn."

He rubbed his chin. "That bed and breakfast is only a few blocks from Patrick's insurance agency. Convenient."

"Why don't we go by there and see if it's true? Someone working there must've seen them," I said.

He bobbed his head. "How are we going to do that without a photo of them?"

"Easy. The internet."

I whipped out my phone from my pocket and went online to search Facebook for Angela's profile. It was set to private, so I searched for Sofia's account, figuring she must have photos of her stepsister. Sofia's profile was public and had tons of photos. I couldn't find one of Angela alone, but I saved a picture of the sisters together. Patrick had commented on Sofia's last post, so I clicked on his name and went to his profile to download a photo of him, too. I wasn't surprised that they were friends since Sofia was his girlfriend's roommate and Patrick and Sofia worked together.

"All set!" I announced. "Let's go."

"You never worked in law enforcement?" Ryker teased. "You seem pretty good at this detective stuff."

"Maybe I was a psychic PI in another life."

"Or maybe you are in this one." He had the cutest crooked grin.

Ryker drove us to the Sleep Inn. He parked on the street in front of a lovely Victorian B&B with a white picket fence and an awning. The wide front porch had two wicker chairs that provided a good spot for observing the foot traffic.

We got out of the Audi and went down a cobblestone path to the front door. Ryker opened it, and I stepped inside. The mostly off-white rooms had high-ceilings, shiny hardwood floors, ceiling fans, and dark wood furnishings. I wrinkled my nose, the space smelling like one of those pine-scented tree air fresheners that people hung from their rearview mirror. Floral artwork and green plants added splashes of vivid color. Fresh flowers sat on a table in the entryway near a grand, curving staircase.

A curvaceous, older woman with green eyes and silver tresses appeared from another room. She wore a simple, blue linen dress with a pink polka-dotted apron tied around her waist.

"Hello! I'm Mrs. Woodhouse. What a lovely couple you two make. Would you like to make a reservation?"

Ryker's neck flushed and I chewed my lip.

"Um, no," I said, recovering faster than Ryker. "Would you mind answering a few questions? We're hoping to clear something up."

"Of course, dear." She stopped beside a tall table with a check-in book resting on it. "What can I help you with?"

I gestured to the book and Ryker nodded. With any luck, Patrick or Angela had registered under their real names.

I stepped further into the room. "What a charming B&B, you have."

"Thank you." Mrs. Woodhouse took the bait and beamed, ushering me into the sitting room on the left. "We've been in business for over thirty years and we have the best breakfast in town," she bragged. "See this Tiffany lamp? It's original to the house built in 1901..."

While she showed off her décor and home, I hoped that

Ryker had gotten my hint and remained behind to leaf through the check-in book to verify that Patrick and Angela had spent time here together. It would prove that either Cassie or Patrick had a motive to kill Angela. Patrick could've killed her if she'd threatened to expose the affair, or if they'd gotten caught by Cassie, then she might've been the one who offed Angela.

I took out my phone and showed Patrick's photo to Mrs. Woodhouse. "Have you seen this man, Patrick Hoang? Does he stay here on occasion?"

"Sorry, but I can't divulge private information."

"Oh, I totally get that," I said. "I'm only asking to help solve the recent murder. You must've heard about it, Angela Hernández died near my grandma's shop—"

"I thought you looked familiar! You must be Danika." She clasped her hands and bounced on her toes. "I'm one of your grandmother's oldest friends."

"I didn't mean to pry, but the sheriff suspects Grandma Elsie of the crime and I just want to clear her name and get justice for Angela."

Mrs. Woodhouse waved a hand in dismissal. "Say no more. Elsie Dreary is a pillar of this community and beloved by all. Just tell me what you need to know, dear."

"Thank you, so, so much!" I showed her the phone again. "Does this man ever stay at the inn?"

Mrs. Woodhouse squinted at the image. "Oh, yes. He stays here twice a month."

I held up my phone with a photo of Sofía and Angela, pointing at Angela. "Has this woman ever been here with Patrick?"

She shook her head. "Never seen her before."

"Are you sure? Please look again."

Mrs. Woodhouse peered closer. "I don't know that woman, but the one beside her is Sofía, Patrick's girlfriend."

The breath hitched in my throat. This was next level cringe. Sofía and Cassie had horizontally tangoed with the same man. And they were friends and roommates.

"Sofía came to this inn with Patrick?" I asked, as if my ears and brain needed confirmation that I'd heard her correctly.

"Many times. They usually request room seven." She started to reenter the foyer.

"Wait!" I said loudly to alert Ryker that we were returning. "When was the last time they were here together?"

Mrs. Woodhouse paused in the archway and scratched her head. "About a week ago. And I'm not one to gossip, but they had a dreadful lover's quarrel. I heard it all the way downstairs and Sofía left before checkout. Poor dears. I suppose they reconciled because he made a reservation for this evening."

"Any idea what they fought about?" I asked.

Mrs. Woodhouse shook her head. "Sorry, dear. I don't know."

She proceeded to the foyer and I followed. Ryker waited by the door, smiling innocently with both hands clasped behind his back. A timer dinged somewhere in the house.

"I have a pie in the oven," Mrs. Woodhouse said. "Do you need anything else, dear?"

"Nope. Thank you for your time." I marched to the door, and Ryker spun on his heel to follow.

Outside, we faced each other by the car.

"Did you get a peek at the book?"

He nodded. "Yup, and you'll never guess what I found."

"Sofía and Patrick's name on the register with a reservation for tonight?"

"Hey! How'd you know that?"

"Because Mrs. Woodhouse told me that Patrick was staying here with Sofía, not Angela. She told me that Patrick and Sofía were bickering the last time they stayed here. She thought Sofía was his girlfriend."

He scratched his chin. "I wonder what they were arguing about. Angela stalking him or his real girlfriend Cassie?"

I shrugged. "Could be both. Seems Patrick Hoang is quite the ladies man."

"With a dead stalker, if it's true."

"Sofía was totally defending his honor at the funeral *and* she's Cassie's roommate."

Ryker blinked. "That's really messed up."

"I know! What should we do now? A stakeout?"

"Sure. We can grab coffee at Brewed Awakening across the street and wait for Patrick to show up and get his side of the story," he said.

"Okay, and we can verify Katherine Harrington's alibi. She claimed she was meeting with a client at the time of the murder."

His mouth twisted in a wry smile. "Do you ever take a pause?"

I grinned. "Only for quesadillas. Mmmm, yummy, cheesy goodness."

We moved the car to a side street and strolled to Brewed Awakening. Inside, we ordered cappuccinos with cookies. We took our treats and mugs, and sat by the bay window.

The aroma of fresh brewed coffee and chocolate delicacies wafted through the coffee shop. Brewed Awakening's interior was warm and inviting, with round tables and hardback chairs. One long counter was stacked with a chrome espresso machine, a whipped cream canister, and colorful coffee mugs. The walls had a rustic appeal decorated in ivory trim with red brick wallpaper. Behind the counter was a blackboard with today's specials. A cushy loveseat was positioned beside a shelf crammed with coffee mugs for sale and free books to read.

Wisps of hazy steam rose from the hot mug. I wrapped both hands around the cup, my tense muscles relaxing as I sipped the delicious coffee. "Mmmm," I murmured, closing my eyes and savoring the rich flavor.

"The coffee here is excellent."

I opened my eyes. "Did you get a chance to talk with Nate? I didn't mean to upset him the other night. I hope he's not angry with me."

Ryker drank his coffee and set it down. "We talked, and Nate understands why you'd suspect his sister. Nate still wants to invite you over for dinner."

"Why?"

"Nate thought you two might work together to discover the truth. He wants to find Angela's killer to clear him of suspicion. And Nate likes you," Ryker said simply.

"Are you going to be there?"

One side of his mouth curled upward. "I could be if you'd like," he said in a low voice that turned my spine soft.

I smiled. "I'd like very much. I don't want to enter hostile territory alone."

"Then I've got your back," he said.

"Can I tell you something?" I asked, smiling shyly.

"Anything."

"I like you, Ryker Van Allen. You're one of the good guys and I'm really glad we're friends."

He leaned back and his cheeks slightly colored. "I am, too. Although, usually when I like a woman, we go on dates—not try to solve a real-life murder."

"How humdrum," I teased.

His stare locked onto mine, and my heart swelled. "Oh, you're anything but boring, Danika Dreary."

We both laughed.

Ryker and I nibbled on our cookies and drank our coffee in comfortable silence, as if we'd been friends for years instead of only weeks. We kept watch out the window at the inn across the street, waiting for Patrick to arrive.

"If Sofía's having an affair with Patrick, why kill Angela?" I said. "You'd think she'd want to kill Cassie and not her stepsister. Sofía had a lot of animosity toward Angela, but is that a strong enough motive for murder?"

Ryker sipped his coffee. "What if Angela discovered the affair? The sisters could've quarreled and the argument got heated and…"

"Then Sofía decides to poison her stepsister." I sighed. "Poison *is* considered a lady's preferred method of killing."

We drank our coffee and he finished off his cookie.

My gaze roamed the space and I decided to check another alibi. "Wait here. I'll be back in a minute."

I stood and slid my phone out of my pocket. I logged into Facebook and searched until I found Katherine Harrington's profile. I zoomed in on her photo and walked up to the counter. Two ladies were working, one refilling the coffeemaker and the other putting fresh pastries on a rack on the counter.

"Excuse me," I said, holding up the phone. "Have either of you seen this woman, Katherine Harrington?"

They both squinted at her photo.

The plump brunette nodded. Her nametag read: *Alice.* "She has coffee here all the time."

I scrolled through my phone, stopping on the image of Sofía and Angela and showed it to her. "Have you seen her with either of these two women?"

Alice nodded. "I know Sofía, she works close by at the insurance agency. It's so horrible what happened to her stepsister. I saw Sofía and Katherine here a few times."

I bobbed my head. "Do you remember ever seeing them together?"

The other woman, a bleached blonde with freckles pulled in her bottom lip, as if thinking. Her name tag said: *Laura*. "Now that I think about it, they were both here the night Angela died. The redhead left when another woman came in."

I showed them the photo again. "Was it this woman? Angela?"

"That's right!" Alice nodded. "They created a huge scene."

"When Angela saw Sofía, she stomped over to her and yelled something about betraying her," Laura said. "Then Patrick Hoang walked in and the three of them started quarreling."

"The manager had to kick them out," Alice said.

"What were they fighting about?" I asked.

"I wasn't really paying attention, but I think one of them said something about infidelity. I'm not sure," Laura said.

Alice shrugged. "I was busy helping customers."

"Thanks for the info." I returned to my seat.

"What did you find out?" Ryker asked.

"It seems Katherine was telling the truth about her whereabouts, which meant she was lying about something else. The women working here said she was here with Sofía. And you said Katherine had a perfume business, right? Could Sofía be a client?"

Was that just a coincidence, or was there a connection to Katherine's business? Every time I'd encountered Sofía, she'd been shrouded in a cloud of perfume so strong it made my nose hair burn. I really wished Sofía would ease up on the scent. My sinuses couldn't take much more of her olfactory assault.

Ryker sipped his coffee. "I didn't even know they knew each other."

An older couple entered the coffee shop, ordered iced coffees, and sat on the loveseat near the bookshelf. The man picked out two paperbacks and handed one to his wife. She grinned at the bodice ripper romance cover. It must be nice to know someone so intimately that you can discern their reading tastes.

My stare met Ryker's soft gaze and he reached across the table to touch my hand. A heated rush of anticipation jolted through me as I laced our fingers. It was a bold move, yet he didn't seem to mind because he smiled. Maybe I was just a lonely woman with an inappropriate crush on her grandma's lawyer.

Across the street Patrick Hoang appeared and he was arguing with a dark-haired woman. She stood in the shadows with her coat hood over her head, concealing her face.

"It's Patrick," Ryker whispered, untangling our fingers. "He's at the inn."

Ah, it was the man who might've driven Cassie or Sofía to commit murder. Or was Patrick their accomplice? Or had he done the deed himself?

"Who's with him? Is it Sofía?" I squinted at the couple standing in front of the Sleep Inn.

Ryker leaned forward and peered through the coffee shop window. "I'm not sure. Let's sneak over there and see."

Eavesdropping had become my middle name.

CHAPTER 21

Ryker and I scrambled out of our seats and left Brewed Awakening. The cool night air embraced us as we hustled along the street to a crosswalk not far from the Sleep Inn. Patrick Hoang and a woman stood arguing on the immaculate green grass of the B&B. We crossed the street and quietly made our way closer to the couple.

Ryker grasped my hand and yanked me behind a massive oak tree with long branches that concealed us from view. He put a finger to his lips and I nodded. I placed a hand on the rough bark and peeked around the trunk. Ryker did the same.

The woman had her back to us and the street, while Patrick faced her. He touched her elbow and she jerked away. She had a dark-brown mane and wore a fur-trimmed coat. The woman held a designer purse in one hand. The scent of pungent vanilla perfume tainted the air—Sofía.

Patrick ran a hand through his black hair. "Don't start again."

"Don't start what?"

"You know exactly *what*. You do this every time we get together lately."

"Not every time," Sofía mumbled.

"Will you just listen to reason for once?" Patrick masked a scowl with a smirk. "I will handle it. I promised, didn't I?"

Sofía sighed, her fingers twitching around the strap of her Fendi purse. "Like how you handled Angela?"

A sickening feeling struck my gut. Did she mean *killed?* I squeezed Ryker's arm.

Patrick threw up his hands. "Do you have to keep bringing her up? Angela's dead."

"It's *over,* Patrick. I'm done."

Sofía whirled to walk away, but he clutched her arm.

"Wait up. Let's talk about it," he pleaded.

She shrugged him off. "There's nothing left to say. I have to go. I left some paperwork at the office. I'll talk to you later." Sofía stomped down the street.

Once she was out of earshot, Ryker and I stepped out from behind the tree. Patrick started toward his Prius with a swaggering strut that even most male models couldn't perfect.

"Hey," Ryker called, waving at him. "Patrick!"

We caught up to him as a Jeep zipped along the road.

"How you doing, Van Allen?" Patrick asked, pausing on the sidewalk. "Still helping little old ladies write up their wills?"

"You know it," Ryker replied.

We reached Patrick, and he eyed us closely, then looked around suspiciously.

"What were you two doing behind that tree? Eavesdropping?" Patrick accused.

"Squirrel hunting," I said quickly.

Patrick looked about with a furrowed brow. "Where are your traps? And why are hunting squirrels?"

"Taxidermy," I said quickly. "I'm looking for dead ones to stuff and add to my collection."

Patrick gazed at me like I was one fry short of a Happy meal. Yes, I know. I'm a terrible liar.

"Never mind that," Ryker said. "Would you like to join us for coffee? I'm buying."

Patrick nodded. "Sure. I could use a cup of joe."

We ambled across the street towards the coffee shop. Patrick barely cast a glance in my direction. I felt kind of shunned and offended, although I wasn't sure why.

The three of us strode into Brewed Awakening and claimed a table near the window facing the street. The older couple was still there, reading their paperbacks and sipping coffee.

Patrick sat across from me at the round table. His black hair was neatly combed and he wore a gray turtleneck under a beige coat with pressed slacks and soft leather loafers. The dark birthmark on his neck peeked out from his collar. He was attractive and knew it. And yet I had an instant dislike of Patrick. Something about him rubbed me the wrong way and it wasn't just because he was cheating on his girlfriend. I thought Cassie should know about his sexual exploits—if she didn't already—but I sure didn't want to be the one to tell her.

Ryker gestured at me. "This is Danika Dreary. She just moved to Mystique—"

"I didn't actually move here," I said. At Ryker's surprised expression, I softened my tone. "I'm only staying with my grandma for a while."

Ryker frowned. "Oh, I thought...never mind." He returned his attention to Patrick. "Do you mind if we ask you a few questions?"

Patrick squinted at the clock on the wall. "I'm running late. There's someone I need to talk to—"

"Sofía Hernández?" Ryker said bluntly.

Patrick stilled, his jaw clenched. "So you were eavesdropping."

I leaned forward. I had no empathy for cheaters or liars. "What if we were?"

A flush shaded Patrick's face and he cracked his knuckles. "It's none of your damn business."

"Settle down," Ryker interjected. "We only want to talk."

Patrick sighed. "Is this some kind of blackmail?"

"Yes, so if you don't talk to us, I'll let the police know about your affair and that would put you at the very top of their suspect list," I said.

Patrick tensed, then shrugged. "Fine. I don't really care. It's over between me and Sofia anyway. She ended it."

"Can you tell us where you were the night Angela died?" Ryker asked.

Patrick leaned back and crossed one leg over his thigh. "I was at work helping a client with insurance on his RV camper."

Truth. Not one icy shiver prickled my neck.

"And how long did that take?" Ryker asked, drumming his fingers on the table. "Can we get the client's name?"

"I've already given all this info to the police and my alibi checked out." Patrick blew out a frustrated breath. "I didn't kill Angela. Why would I?"

My nape stayed warm. He was speaking the truth.

"Okay," I said. "Then does Cassie know about the affair? Is that why Sofia ended it with you tonight?"

Patrick grunted. "No one knows except you two about me and Sofia. How'd you find out, anyway?"

Ryker smirked and our eyes met. "Danika's one heck of a detective."

"Oh, yeah?" Patrick cocked his head. "You work for the police?"

I snorted and slouched in my seat. "Nope. I co-own Karma Moon."

"That detached from reality witchcraft store?" Patrick said with a brittle laugh. "Those hipster airheads are absurd—"

"Hey, now!" I sat up straight. My whole body warmed with indignation. "There's nothing wrong with seeking enlightenment, or the power of positive thinking, or feeling grateful for the people and things in your life."

I inhaled a staggering breath, but it stuck in my throat. What was up with me? I was defending Karma Moon like a mama bear protecting a cub.

Patrick raised both hands to ward me off. "Chill out. I didn't realize you were one of those Wiccan chicks."

"I'm not a witch," I said with a sugary smile. "But I am smart."

He uncrossed his legs and pushed back his chair. "I dunno about that. You're weird like your grandmother."

I could feel the blood rushing to my head. Clamping my mouth shut, I glowered at Patrick.

The elderly woman and her husband sitting across the room shot Patrick a disapproving scowl, then went back to reading their books. But I could tell the by the tilt of the woman's head that she was listening to our conversation.

Ryker stood up so fast, his chair flew back and thumped against the wall. "Apologize."

Patrick waved flippantly at him. "Okay, okay. I'm sorry. That kind of stuff just makes me uncomfortable."

Ryker retook his seat. "Is it true that Angela was stalking you?"

"Yeah, she was annoying," Patrick admitted. "I got fed up with her weirdness and went to talk to Sofia about it since we work together and they were stepsisters. I asked Sofia to talk some damn sense into Angela."

Truth. None of the little hairs on my neck tingled. This was a waste of time.

"Why don't you breakup with Cassie?" I blurted. "Why cheat on her?"

Patrick was quiet a moment, then laced his fingers and cracked his knuckles again. "I love her, and Sofía's just sex. I know how that sounds, but the point is, I didn't poison Angela."

All true. My sixth sense didn't even prickle.

Patrick's phone chimed and he slipped it out of his pocket. He touched the green button. "Hello?" He was silent, listening to the caller. "I'll be right there." He stood. "We're done here." The womanizing Patrick left the coffee shop.

"Was he lying about anything?" Ryker asked.

I shook my head. "Nope. He was telling the truth."

"That narrows down our suspect list. Another coffee?" Ryker asked.

"Sure."

He went to the counter to order, while I contemplated what Patrick had revealed.

The smug jerk had been honest and unwavering in his answers. The killer had to be either Cassie or Sofía. But then there was Katherine Harrington, Nate's snobby sister. She could've killed Angela, too. Although her alibi had checked out, Katherine could've poisoned that love potion at any time. I'd have to take Nate up on that dinner invitation to get the truth.

I had narrowed it down to three female suspects, but I still strongly felt like Cassie had the biggest motive, availability, and opportunity. Cassie had no real alibi and she hated Angela more than anyone. And if Cassie was the murderer, what would she do when she caught Sofía and Patrick? I shuddered to think about more deaths.

The older woman sitting across from me raised her head and grinned. I halfheartedly returned it.

Sirens blared. A police car and ambulance zoomed past the window. I jumped to my feet. Ryker and I ran outside. The vehicles screeched to a halt three blocks away and across the street in front of Patrick's insurance agency. The paramedics rushed into the office.

Was it Patrick? He'd just left the coffee shop.

Ryker and I wandered closer. A stuttering streetlamp glinted in the night as the medics rolled out a woman on a gurney.

CHAPTER 22

Sofía lay on the gurney, moaning and clutching her stomach. White foam coated her lips. It looked as if she had been poisoned like Angela.

Deputy Reid led Patrick out of the insurance agency in handcuffs.

"Stay here," Ryker whispered. "I know one of the paramedics. I'll try to find out what happened." He left me on the sidewalk a block away and went over to the ambulance.

Patrick was shoved into the police car, bellowing how he was innocent. Deputy Reid spotted me huddled under the awning of an antique store and scowled. Then the grumpy deputy got into the cruiser and sped off.

After the ambulance drove away, a slip of paper on the ground tumbled in the breeze and landed at my feet. I crouched to pick it up—a deposit slip for cash with Sofía's name on it in the amount of five thousand dollars.

Not suspicious at all.

Covertly, I inserted the slip into my pocket.

Ryker returned and ushered me back to the coffee shop. We retook our seats near the window.

"What happened?" I asked, wrapping my hands around my warm mug. "Is Patrick the killer?"

The older couple still lounged by the bookshelves, reading and sipping their drinks.

Ryker tilted his head to the side. "From what I gathered, Patrick got a phone call from Sofia and went to his office. He found her passed out on the floor with a coffee mug beside her. The paramedics think Sofia's been poisoned. I think Patrick is the sheriff's lead suspect now, but he wasn't officially charged with anything yet."

I reclined in my seat. "It seems odd that Patrick called for an ambulance if he was attempting to poison Sofia."

"I guess we can cross her off our suspect list."

"What if Cassie knew about Sofia and Patrick's affair? And she tried to kill Sofia? We found the voodoo doll in the back of Patrick's car with dark hairs stitched into it."

Ryker rubbed his chin. "That makes Cassie our top suspect."

I extracted the deposit slip from my pocket. "I found this outside of the insurance agency. It has Sofia's name on it."

He whistled. "Wow. That's a hefty sum of money."

"Was Patrick paying Sofia in cash?"

"I highly doubt it. Patrick told me once that he kept detailed records on everything. He'd never pay anyone under the table." Ryker's cell rang and pushed away from the table. "Be back in a minute." He went outside to answer the call.

The elderly couple sitting across from us were whispering and peeking over at me. I didn't think I knew them, but Grandma Elsie probably did. The woman ambled over to me. She had kind eyes and a full head of gunmetal-gray hair. She reminded me of a schoolteacher I'd had in sixth grade. Her clothes were modest, a cotton blouse, rayon slacks, and beige orthopedic shoes.

"Good evening, sweetie. I couldn't help overhearing your conversation. I'm Yvette Hickson and I used to work at the bank." She pointed at the man. "That's my husband Jerold."

I waved at Jerold. "Hello."

"It's awful what happened to Angela and now her sister," Yvette said, her voice raspy. She pointed at the deposit slip on the table. "If Sofia dies, I wonder what's going to happen to all that money now."

My brows crinkled. "What do you mean?"

Yvette shifted her weight and chewed her lip. "I really shouldn't discuss it. Even former employees aren't supposed to talk about the bank's clients and their finances."

Hmmm. Then why did she bring it up? She looked like she was dying to share some juicy town gossip.

"You can trust me," I said. "It'll just be between us. Do you know something about Angela's murder?"

"Not directly," Yvette whispered. "While I was still working at the bank before I retired, you see, Sofia was making these large monthly deposits in cash."

"She was? How long was she doing that? Was it recent?"

"Oh, for about six months. I thought she'd won the lottery, but it was never announced on the news. I tried to ask her where she was getting all this money, but she wouldn't tell me and even called me a meddlesome old lady!"

"Maybe Sofia has a side hustle and gets paid in cash."

Yvette quirked her head. "Possibly, but I still think it's odd."

I remembered Sofia coming by the store and complaining that she only had one-hundred dollar bills stuffed into her bra.

"That is strange," I agreed. "But I'm not sure why you're telling me this..."

Yvette gave me a knowing nod. "I thought you might be

interested is all. We know Elsie Dreary didn't harm Angela." She leaned in closer and lowered her voice. "I told Sheriff Hall about the money, but he didn't seem concerned."

"And you think the murder and the deposits are somehow related?"

"That's for you to determine, sweetie." Yvette shrugged. "Tell Elsie we'll see her at the next church bake sale." She shuffled back to her seat.

Ryker returned. "Ready to go?"

"Yeah. Would you mind taking me home?"

He slowly smiled. "Home?"

I felt my cheeks heat. "I meant to my grandma's shop."

On the way back to Karma Moon, I told him what Yvette had said about Sofia making those big cash deposits. "What if Sofia was blackmailing someone? And perhaps Angela got involved?"

His hands tightened on the steering wheel. "I'm not sure what to think, but it does seem incongruous."

Although, Patrick was in custody and suspected of both poisonings, he'd been truthful when Ryker and I had questioned him. I couldn't help feeling the police had made a mistake and the real killer was still out there.

When Ryker parked at the curb to let me out, I shifted to face him.

"Goodnight, Ryker."

"Sweet dreams, Danika," he said, his voice soft and deep.

I got out and Ryker drove away. The streetlight between the shop and Ryker's law firm was out, pitching the alley into inky darkness. I went to the front of the shop and tried the door, but had the wrong key.

Using the flashlight on my phone, I ventured into the alleyway. The security light over the back door was off. The beam from my cell didn't cast much brightness as I scurried to the door. My shoes crunched over broken glass. A heavy feeling settled in my gut. The lightbulb was broken.

As I stuck the key in the lock, someone stepped out of the dark, but I couldn't see their face.

"You know what they say about curious cats in Mystique?" a deep voice rumbled from the darkness. "They tend to run out of their nine lives real quick."

The intruder shoved me hard into the door, and I stumbled. Adrenaline pumping, I caught myself on the frame with both hands. Spinning about, I went to confront them, but the person sprinted out of the alley and into the night.

CHAPTER 23

THE FIRST THING I DID WAS CHECK ON GRANDMA Elsie, who was dozing with a book beside her in bed, and decided not to wake her. After making sure that every entrance to the shop was locked tight, I contacted Sheriff Hall about the threat I'd received from an unknown assailant. Since I hadn't seen the person, I couldn't offer much of a description. The sheriff told me to come by the station to give a statement. I hung up, then crammed my clothes into the dresser and closet. The empty suitcases got shoved in the back, where they'd probably stay until my next crisis.

I pondered the warning to stop investigating Angela's murder. I would've guessed Patrick had been the culprit, but he'd just been arrested. Or perhaps it was Gideon Harrington. Or Weatherby on Gideon's behalf. It couldn't be Cassie because the person had sounded like a male and was much taller. My numero uno suspects had been femme fatales—Cassie and Sofia. Then my throat felt thick. Maybe I'd been very wrong all this time and the killer had been a man all along.

So who had rudely threatened me to quit solving the crime? Not a darn clue.

What would I do now, you ask? You guessed it. Keep investigating.

I finally fell asleep around three am. When I awoke the next day, I ventured into the kitchen and told Grandma Elsie over breakfast about my late-night visitor, Sofia's poisoning, and Patrick being arrested. "What do you think?"

Grandma Elsie rubbed her lucky rabbit's foot in one hand. "I still believe Cassie and Patrick are innocent. Arrested isn't the same as guilty,"

"True. But I disagree. Patrick might've been arrested, but Cassie still looks pretty guilty."

"That may be true, sweetheart, but the killer is never the obvious suspect," Grandma Elsie said.

"I was thinking since Gideon Harrington told me to stop investigating that maybe it was his majordomo, Weatherby, that tried to scare me off the case."

She nodded. "You might be right. I wouldn't put it past that family. Now put your Sherlock Holmes's cap away, it's time to open Karma Moon."

Grandma Elsie might've been right. I was hyper-focused on Cassie as the murderer. She was the obvious suspect and had the strongest motive, but that didn't mean she was guilty. I had to talk with her again and get to the truth of her alibi.

Throughout the day, I had an uncomfortable feeling crawl along my spine. I kept scanning the shop and looking out the windows anxiously. It felt like someone was stalking me, like my every move was being scrutinized. Maybe whoever had threatened me was making sure I quit investigating.

During my lunch break, I texted Ryker to meet me for coffee. We sat at the same table in Brewed Awakening as the last time. A hipster couple lounged on the loveseat talking and guzzling shots of expresso.

Ryker and I ordered mochas. I noted he looked really good in a black V-neck shirt and jeans.

"Not working today?" I asked, gesturing at his casual attire.

"I took the afternoon off. So tell me why you wanted to meet."

He sipped his drink while I told him what happened the previous evening after he'd dropped me off.

"Do you think Cassie has a male accomplice, who threatened me?"

Ryker dabbed at his mouth with a napkin from the metal dispenser on the table. "It's possible. And here I hoped the case was closed, but I realize being arrested doesn't mean Patrick was guilty of the crime."

"I wonder how Sofia's doing." I yawned and sipped my coffee. I hadn't slept much and a jolt of caffeine was in order. "Can you call Nate to arrange that dinner he offered to host?"

"Why?"

"It's a gut feeling," I said. "I can't explain it, and while Patrick and Cassie seem like the obvious suspects, I need hard evidence to give the police."

"I get it. You want to rule out all the innocent people and have solid proof that points to the murderer. Does next Saturday night work for you? The Harringtons usually dine at seven."

"That would be perfect," I said. "Do wanna drive over together?"

"Sure. I'll pick you up at six-thirty." Ryker bit into his pastry and swallowed. "You sure about this? Whoever threatened you might follow through on their warning."

I sipped my hot drink. "It's a chance I'll take to uncover what really happened to Angela."

"Did you tell Sheriff Hall about the threat?" he asked.

"I did. He said to come by the station to give a statement, but since I didn't get a good look at the person, I really don't see the point."

"I still think you should talk to the police." Ryker withdrew his phone from a pocket and started texting someone. "I'll have Nate invite his sister to dinner, along with Cassie and Patrick."

My stomach tightened. We'd be dining with a possible killer and their accomplice—what could possibly go wrong? Don't answer that.

"Patrick's not in jail?" My voice sounded pitchy.

Ryker shook his head, still focused on the phone. "I heard he was questioned, but released because they didn't have enough evidence to hold him."

"Does Nate know Patrick and Cassie?"

"Patrick insures the Harrington family's cars, homes, and life insurance policies. He's been to the manor many times with Cassie. So they all know each other, but I wouldn't exactly call them friends," Ryker said. "Patrick has had dinner there before, and I'm sure Nate won't mind inviting them. He likes your grandma and wants to help."

"It'll be an interesting evening. Do you think Nate would mind inviting Sofia, too? If she's out of the hospital by then. Or would that be weird?"

"There might be pushback from the elder Harringtons, but Nate can convince them. Besides, Sofia's stepmother has worked for the family for years." Ryker finished texting and put his phone away. His hand reached across the table to touch the back of mine and a nice shiver tingled over my skin. "What do you hope to gain by having everyone come to dinner?"

"Maybe I can trap one of them into a confession and get their real alibis. I know Cassie and Sofia were lying about something. And having all of them in one room should finally expose the truth."

Ryker finished his coffee. "I have some errands to run. Be careful, will ya?"

"Always. See you soon."

I sat there a while and watched cars and people passing by the window. A contented feeling I'd never felt before overcame me and I smiled.

As much as I didn't want to admit it, I really liked it here. I realized how lonely and meaningless my life had been, especially after spending the last few weeks in Mystique. It had taken the loss of a job, boyfriend, and roommate for me to find good friends and an occupation I was starting to love. It felt gratifying to help the customers in the shop. And to have found a place where people truly cared about me and my grandma, who wanted to help solve a murder without wanting anything in return.

My twenties were a blur of room rentals, short-term sublets, and couch surfing. Now into my early thirties, I was getting tired of completely uprooting my life and having to start anew every couple of years. I was also sick of living paycheck-to-paycheck. Grandma Elsie was offering me a precious gift—a home and a steady income. Two things sorely lacking in my nomad lifestyle.

For the first time, I'd actually found a place where I could see myself happily settling down. But would I? I still wasn't one-hundred percent sure.

Then I thought of Ryker and my attraction to the handsome lawyer. How could a relationship built on a murder mystery ever be appropriate?

My mind wandered back to the Harrington dinner where all the suspects would be dining in one place. My plan had the potential for absolute disaster, like a family picnicking on the train tracks. So, yeah, this probably wouldn't end well.

CHAPTER 24

A WEEK HAD PASSED SINCE PATRICK HAD BEEN arrested as a suspect and released, and Sofía had been discharged from the hospital. Word on the street was that Sofía hadn't ingested enough poison to be fatal and she had gone home after two days. Sofía would make a full recovery. With my first paycheck, I sent her "get well" flowers through Lucinda's shop.

The clock on the nightstand revealed I had ten minutes until Ryker arrived to escort me to the Harrington Manor for dinner. And I still couldn't decide what to wear.

Sashay lay sprawled on the bed as I stared at myself in the full-length mirror. I had arranged my pink hair into a cute updo, and chosen a semi-formal royal-blue dress that fell above the knee. The stretch-jersey material hugged my curves and featured a floral-lace overlay with a scalloped V-neckline, exposing a hint of cleavage. Not too racy or conservative.

"What do you think, Sashay?" I turned to the adorable gray feline.

The cat yawned and closed her eyes. Sashay was obviously as bored with my outfit changes as I was. This dress would have to do. Looking pristine wasn't only something I wasn't interested in, but dressing up made me feel downright out of place. Seriously, being in a room full of faces with flawlessly applied makeup and not a hair in disarray was, basically, my own personal hell.

I slipped on a pair of strappy, two-inch heels, and spritzed myself with a pear-scented body spray. Then I brushed my hair, smelling of apricot mousse and Pantene. The final touch was applying my makeup: lots of mascara and my signature red lipstick.

Tonight would change everything. The killer was joining us for dinner, I knew it in my bones. All I had to do was get to the truth, which would narrow down my suspects. I could do this, right? *Right!* Detective Danika Dreary was on the case. That had a nice ring to it, don't you think?

My phone pinged with a text and I lifted it off the bed. Ryker waited downstairs. I texted back that I'd be down in five minutes, and selected a glittery handbag from the closet, then shoved my keys, lipstick, and phone inside.

I paused in the archway dividing the hallway from the living room, where Grandma Elsie sat on the sofa consulting her tarot cards spread out on the coffee table.

"Are you sure this dinner is a good idea, sweetheart?" she asked, her face pinched. "It might be dangerous."

I entered the room, gripped my grandma's hand, and squeezed it. "Please don't worry, Nana. This is just something I need to see through to the end."

Someone had murdered Angela and let my grandma look guilty, albeit briefly, and that was all kinds of wrong. Whoever did this deserved to pay for their crimes.

Grandma Elsie leaned back on the sofa. "Please be careful."

"I will. I love you, Nana."

"I love you too, sweetheart."

I waved goodbye and descended the spiral staircase into the storeroom. I went out the back door and through the alley. Ryker waited outside near his car.

Holy hot tamales—he looked good enough to eat. My heart fluttered at the sight of him in a button-up white shirt under a black blazer with slacks.

His soft brown eyes lit up when he saw me. I smiled. The dress had been a good choice after all.

"Hi," I said almost shyly.

"Wow. You're a vision," Ryker said, grinning, and then gesturing at himself. "Should I go home and change?"

"No need. You look incredibly handsome."

The compliment only widened his smile. Ryker opened the car door and I slid onto the seat. After shutting it, he went around and jumped in. We made small talk on the drive over.

When we arrived at La Casa de Harrington, Ryker parked behind Patrick's Prius in front of the mansion. We got out and walked to the stairs. He reached for my hand and laced our fingers. My skin tingled and flushed at his warm grip. Ryker paused on the porch before the front door.

"Do we need a safe word?"

I giggled. "In case things get too intense?"

He quirked a brow. "Or murderous," he said in an ominous tone.

"That's not funny." I frowned. "We don't know if Patrick or Cassie are guilty or innocent yet."

"True. So safe word?"

"Chalupa."

"Nice." Ryker's hand still held mine and he gave it a gentle squeeze, then let go. "Ready?"

My heart was beating hard and fast. I took a deep breath, then blew it out. Straightening my shoulders, I gave myself a mental pep-talk. I was a formidable, formidable woman. Strong and fierce. Ready to unleash my inner-detective and takedown killers. And to be perfectly honest, this investigator work was actually exciting.

I nodded and straightened my dress. "Ready."

Ryker rang the doorbell. A minute later, the double-doors swung wide and Weatherby stood in the entrance.

He bowed curtly at Ryker and ignored me. The tall, willowy fellow wore a tweed suit straight out of a British sitcom and his full beard had streaks of gray that partially concealed his thin lips.

"Excellent to see you again, Mr. Van Allen. Please follow me," Weatherby said.

Ryker and I trailed after Weatherby through the grand foyer with marble flooring. An extravagant staircase rose to a balcony overlooking the first floor. On the left was a lavish parlor in ivory and on the right a billiard room. Everywhere I looked gleamed polished mahogany, priceless knick-knacks, luxurious furnishings, paintings in ornate gold frames, and crystal chandeliers.

Weatherby led us into a formal dining room with a table long enough to seat twenty people. The gray textured wallpaper created a stylish complement to the intricate white wainscoting and crown molding. I started to feel uncomfortable in such an extravagant room. Afraid to even touch anything.

"You look nervous. Nothing in here will bite you," Ryker teased.

I gave him a sideways glance. "Easy for you to say. You could probably afford to replace anything you break, while I'll be slaving away for decades just to pay off a broken water glass."

"The Harringtons aren't *that* bad. They're only a little evil on Friday nights during a full moon," he joked.

But I didn't laugh. The Ravenscrofts seemed shady. They totally reeked of, well, shadiness.

Ryker tucked his hand lightly around my waist, leading me into a room big enough to host an entire football team. I tried not to gawk at the silk upholstered dining chairs, sleek table, and sparkling chandelier. Dark red drapes framed two floor-to-ceiling windows and a maroon area rug covered most of the polished hardwood floor. A hearth with a crackling fire was on the same wall as a built-in bar. A dozen long-stemmed roses in a crystal vase sat in the center of the table.

Cassie and Patrick stood by the fireplace, holding wine glasses. They appeared tense and alert. Maybe wondering why they'd been invited to dinner. Patrick wore a dark-blue suit and tie. Cassie looked pretty in a lavender blouse and black rayon pants with her butterscotch-colored ringlets swept off her face. She gave me a little wave hello and I nodded.

Nate, wearing a somber gray suit and slacks, reached two fingers under his eyeglasses to rub his eyes. His sister, Katherine, draped in a white dress, hovered near the bar refilling a wine glass from a decanter. Her red waves were styled into a low ponytail at the nape of her neck.

Sofía stood alone near the windows. Her dark tresses were twisted up on top of her head and she'd squeezed her voluptuous figure into a gaudy, gold-sequined dress.

Sheesh. This was dinner, not the Oscars.

Sofía scampered over to me and grabbed me in a rib-crushing hug before I had a chance to hold my breath. I wrinkled my nose. Sofía's perfume was as strong as ever, dealing a heavy blow to my sinuses.

"How are you feeling?" I asked.

Sofía waved a dismissive hand in the air. "Perfectly fine, chica. I got lucky, the doctors said I hadn't ingested enough poison to be lethal. I'd only taken a few sips when I noticed a bitter taste in my coffee. If I'd drunk any more, you'd be attending my funeral about now."

"Hey, Sofía," Ryker said. "Did the doctors say if the poison was the same one that killed your stepsister?"

"Was it Tanas Root?" I added.

Sofía glanced around as if she had the juiciest gossip to share and wanted to sprinkle it out to savor every morsel. "It was, and I know who spiked the coffee. It was Cassie," she said, casting a hard look in her archenemy's direction.

"Are you sure? What if someone else had it out for you and Angela?" I said. "Aren't you worried?"

"Well, I wasn't until now!" Sofía exclaimed, placing a hand flat on her ample chest.

"Can you think of anyone besides Cassie who would've wanted to poison you?" Ryker asked.

"Haven't a damn clue." Sofía's voice wobbled and her hand dropped to her side.

Lies! My neck felt frosty, like a bag of ice pressed against my skin. Sofía did have someone else in mind, but she wasn't sharing.

"Look, let's cutout the pleasantries," I said. "Do you want to confess to killing Angela? Just tell us the truth."

"Are you nuts? Why would I kill Angela?" Sofía said, her mouth twisting into a frown.

I shrugged. "You know, sibling rivalry and all that."

"Oh." She nodded. "I guess that makes sense, but I didn't kill her. I can't believe you suspected me, chica!" Sofía playfully socked me in the shoulder.

Truth. No chilliness on my neck. Ryker raised an eyebrow and I shook my head to indicate she wasn't lying.

"Sorry, but I had to ask," I said, feeling bad for accusing her.

"It's okay," Sofía said. "I might've suspected me, too."

Ryker stayed close by my side, his arm and shoulder brushing against mine. I liked having him near me. He provided a sense of safety and comfort. It was reassuring to know I wasn't alone in my quest to bring a killer to justice.

Sofía leaned closer to me. Her noxious perfume invaded my senses and I tried not to grimace.

"I moved back in with my papa and stepmother, Maria, after I left the hospital. I just couldn't go back and live with Cassie another second," Sofía said.

"Because of Patrick?" Ryker whispered.

"No because I'm pretty sure Cassie was the one who poisoned me," Sofía replied, then changed the subject. "I'm not entirely sure why Nate invited me. We barely know each other, but I couldn't turn down a chance to get a peek at this house."

I stepped back. "It's impressive, but I was the one who asked Nate to invite you to dinner tonight."

Sofía tilted her head. "Why's that?"

I couldn't exactly admit that the dinner was a ruse to catch the killer, who I believed would be dining with us. A social gathering was the perfect opportunity to find out the truth while everyone's guard would be down. Eating and drinking tended to do that.

"Because of everything you've been through, I thought a lovely dinner with friends would be a nice distraction," I said.

"Oh, Danika! That's so sweet," she cooed.

Ryker asked if I wanted any wine, and I said no. I had to stay clearheaded. He excused himself to say hello to the other guests.

Weatherby went to the bar to pour a drink.

Gideon strode into the room wearing a swanky black, three-piece suit with a blue silk shirt. Sofía stiffened at the sight of him. Maybe because his very presence commanded the room. Everyone turned to look at Gideon as he paused in the doorway and yanked at his cuffs.

Weatherby handed Gideon a scotch on the rocks in a sweaty glass, then exited the room. As Gideon sauntered past Sofía and me, he sneered. Guess he wasn't joining my fan club anytime soon. Gideon sat at one end of the table and sipped his scotch.

"Do you know if Nate's mother is joining us?" I asked.

Sofía shook her head. "Nate said his mother, Eleanor, is resting upstairs in her suite. Something about a headache or menstrual cramps, I forget which."

I wondered if Eleanor shared the other Harringtons' hatred for the Dreary family. I gripped Sofía's elbow and moved us away from the others to talk more privately.

"Can I ask you one more question, Sofía?" I said. "The night of Angela's murder, where you at home watching TV with Cassie?"

Sofía rocked on her heels and her shoulders slumped. "Not exactly. I met Katherine for coffee, then Angela showed up. She was all salty and wanted to talk to me, so Katherine left. Then Angela and I had a nasty squabble."

"What did Angela want to talk about?" I stared at her, then lowered my voice. "She knew about you and Patrick, didn't she?"

Sofía nodded, tears lining her eyes. "Angela found a receipt in my coat pocket for the Sleep Inn and staked the place out. One night, she saw me with Patrick there and she took photos of us together. Angela was obsessed with Patrick and even threatened to tell Cassie if I didn't end it."

"What did you do?"

"Patrick showed up and the three of us got into a horrible fight. The manager of the coffee shop told us to leave. I went home and watched a movie with Cassie, then went to bed. The next day, I found out Angela was dead."

All true.

From the corner of my eye, I spied Patrick leaving the room.

"Why were you meeting Katherine? And who do you *really* think tried to poison you?"

"I'll explain later, chica," Sofía said distractedly.

She didn't deign to answer my questions. Suspicious? Oh, yeah.

"No, *now*," I insisted, gripping her arm.

Sofía shook me off. "Katherine wanted my help with something so she'd stay anonymous, okay? She gave me a case of free perfume. It was no big deal."

"Did that have anything to do with those big cash deposits you were making at the bank? I found one of your bank slips."

"Yes, but I can't talk about that here." She glanced at Katherine and took off after Patrick.

My tête-à-tête with Sofía only created more questions. But there was one other person here that I had to interrogate.

CHAPTER 25

Since I'd finished questioning Sofía for the moment, I made a beeline for Cassie standing on the other side of the dining room. Nate was busy conversing with Ryker and Katherine. As I passed Ryker, he gave me a chin nod.

"Hi, Cassie," I said. "Where did Patrick go?"

"To the bathroom," she said. "I didn't know you knew the Harringtons."

"Just Nate..." I swallowed and decided to be blunt. "I know you lied about spending the entire evening with Sofía the night Angela was poisoned. Did you kill her?"

Cassie propped her fists on her slender hips. "*No!*"

I crossed my arms. "Then what were you really doing? And don't lie to me, I'll know if you are."

"Oh? Is that so?" Cassie lowered her arms and pushed a curl off her forehead. "I was waxing my legs."

Coldness tingled at the back of my neck. "Lie."

"That was too easy." She smirked, tapping a finger against her lips. "Tell me which is the lie...I love fried okra and I'm an expert baton twirler."

"Both are true."

Cassie gazed down at me through narrowed eyes. "How? What?—"

"Quiet." I shushed her. "You can confess now. Tell the truth. Get it off your chest..."

She twirled a curl around her finger. "You're saying, I can share my secret?" she asked in a soft voice.

I nodded. *Finally!* Cassie would confess to the murder and I'd call Sheriff Hall. I'd be the town hero. They might even throw a parade in my honor.

"Yes. Tell me everything."

"Okay, well, I participate in LARPing once a month in Ripon," she said.

My nape stayed warm.

I frowned. "What does that have to do with the murder? And what is tarping?"

"Murder? Nothing." A flush colored her neck and ears. "But it's LARPing, *not* tarping. It's a live action role-playing game, where adults dress up in costumes. Right now we're reenacting King Arthur in medieval times."

All true. While I had no idea what she was talking about, it sounded fun. But there had to be something I was missing. I needed her to own up to the killing.

"Why would you lie about that?" I asked.

She hung her head. "Because Patrick makes fun of me and I get embarrassed about it. But it's just something I do for myself that I don't like to share with other people," Cassie said, keeping her voice low. "Anyway, the night Angela died, I got home around six o'clock. Sofia arrived shortly after I did and we watched a movie together."

Truth. Not a trace of coldness on my skin.

"So just to be clear, you didn't kill Angela and try to poison Sofia?"

Cassie's nose wrinkled and her eyes went wide. "Of

course not! Sure, I'm upset that Sofía moved out, but I would never hurt her. She owes me back rent and she can't pay me if she's dead."

Again, my skin stayed warm. Darn. I'd been wrong this whole time. Cassie was innocent.

I had everyone's real alibi now, but I still had no idea who the killer might be. My assumption that it was a man after the threat I'd received could've been correct, but who had wanted Angela dead? If not Patrick, then I was at a loss as to who else might've had motive and opportunity.

Sensing eyes boring into my skull, I spun around. Mrs. Blanche Harrington, Nate's grandmother, looked regal in an indigo blazer over a silk blouse and pants with precious jewels adorning her neck and ears. She stood behind a chair at one end of the table, eyeing her motley group of unwanted guests. Her short, silver hair framed a pallid face. Mrs. Harrington's gray stare scanned me from head-to-toe and her lips thinned into a dark-red line.

I squirmed and my body heat rose under such scrutiny. At some point, I'd have to get my grandma and Blanche together to call a dang truce all ready. This family war had to end, but tonight it could wait.

"Excuse me, everyone," Mrs. Harrington said in a loud, authoritative voice. "Please be seated."

Patrick reentered the room, straightening his tie. A moment later, Sofía flounced in, fluffing her hair. I cringed. Please tell me those two weren't hooking up in some random bedroom.

Sofía started to take a seat near Mrs. Harrington.

The older woman wrinkled her nose. "What in the devil are you doing?" Mrs. Harrington shooed Sofía away with both jeweled hands. "Have a seat at the far end, your fragrance annoys me. Have you never heard the term, '*less is more*'?"

Sofia's face colored a bright red and she shuffled away to take a seat by Patrick. Poor Sofia. Now that she wasn't a suspect, I'd invite her out to lunch. It was obvious she needed a friend.

Taking a seat, I studied the room as I unfolded a linen napkin and placed it on my lap. Mrs. Harrington took a seat at the end of the table opposite Gideon. Across from me were Cassie, Patrick, and Sofia. On my side, Katherine sat beside Nate. Ryker was seated on Mrs. Harrington's left, with me on his right.

The first course was served by two women in black uniforms. A bowl of Italian pasta soup was placed in front of each guest, followed by a golden raisin and broccoli salad. I was a little nervous about dining with a possible poisoner, so I only pushed the food around on my plate.

Everyone ate in unnerving silence. Talk about awkward with a capital A.

"Sooo," I said. "Sofia, how do you know everyone?"

"Cassie was friends with my stepsister in high school, and she's my roommate. I met Patrick at the insurance agency where we work together," Sofia said, casting a quick glance at her roommate and secret lover. "And I've bumped into Nate and Ryker at the coffee shop."

"What about the other Harringtons?" I asked.

"This is the first time I've officially met them," Sofia replied.

A zap of cold smacked my nape. Lies. But why? Her stepmother worked for the Harringtons for a gazillion years so it wouldn't be odd that Sofia might've met them before tonight.

"Don't you mean *former* roommate since you moved out while I was at work," Cassie accused, glaring hard at Sofia. "You owe me a month's rent!"

"You know, Cassie," Sofía said with a smirk, "you'll make a great first wife someday."

"Ladies! The cat fight can wait until after dinner," Ryker said sternly.

"My money's on Sofía for the win," Katherine said with a wink.

The conversation was rapidly turning into an ugly shade throwing squabble. Time for a subject change.

I caught Katherine's eye. "I heard you own a perfume company."

"That's right," Katherine said. "Sofía is wearing one of my most popular fragrances."

Sofía bounced in her seat. "I am? You created *Kiss My Scent*? It's beautiful."

Katherine's lips puckered. "It is, honey, but you need to use it *sparingly*."

Nate raised one hand to shove his glasses more firmly onto his nose. "Sis, don't be rude to our guests."

Katherine shrugged and took a sip of wine. Mrs. Harrington's lips curved into a taunting sneer. Gideon chuckled. Ryker kept eating. Patrick drank from his water glass and Cassie wiped at the corners of her mouth with a napkin. I felt bad for Sofía and gave her a sympathetic smile.

"Oh, yeah, okay," Sofía mumbled, hanging her head.

"It smells fantastic on you," Nate said soothingly.

Sofía lifted her face and faintly smiled at Nate.

Weatherby appeared and whispered into Mrs. Harrington's ear. She stood and addressed the guests. "I'm afraid I need to cut dinner short. I have to take a call from the Mystique Historical Society. I'm hosting this month's fundraiser."

Mrs. Harrington excused herself and exited the room with

the majordomo. Gideon got to his feet and poured himself more scotch, then retook his seat.

Sofía stabbed her fork into her salad and took a bite. She swallowed and cast a glance at Nate, twisting in her seat to face him. "Thank you for inviting me." A piece of broccoli poked out from her front teeth. "I'm really enjoying myself."

Nate took off his glasses. "Your most welcome, Sofía. Angela was a bit of a question mark, but I liked her. And I wanted to pay my respects. Danika thought a dinner would be a nice way to do that."

Cassie settled her fork on the plate. "Angela and I were close in high school, then she changed. She always suffered from jealousy and pigheadedness, except she took it to another level when she set her sights on Patrick—"

"We shouldn't be discussing this," Patrick reprimanded.

"Why not?" Cassie asked. "Not like it's a big secret in this small town."

Ah, but there were still *some* secrets, like his affair with Sofía. I looked at Patrick and he shifted in his seat, trying to avoid my accusing stare.

"Everyone knows Angela was hassling me and stalking you," Cassie said, tears lining her eyes. "Now you're a suspect in her murder. It's totally ridiculous, I tell you. *Ridiculous!*"

Nate put his glasses back on, lifted his fork and pointed it at Patrick. "What motive would you have to kill Angela?"

Patrick cleared his throat. "None. I felt sorry for her. It's obvious she was unstable and needed professional help."

My neck was room temperature, which meant Patrick was being truthful.

"Enough." Gideon raised his water glass. "A toast to Angela. May she rest in peace."

Everyone lifted a glass and mumbled the same sentiment.

The two women returned and took away the dishes,

replacing them with the entrée—a slice of honey-glazed ham with russet potatoes and yellow squash dripping in a buttery sauce. I graciously thanked them, and the women departed.

María Hernández strode into the room and Sofía jumped up from her seat.

"Maria? What're you doing here?" Sofía moved around the table to stand next to her stepmother.

Maria was a plump woman with a pretty face. She wore a drab, amaretto-brown dress with black stockings and low heels. In one hand, she clutched a document.

Maria confronted the guests. "*Buenas noches*, everyone. Sorry to interrupt your feast." Her gaze focused on Gideon. "Can you tell me what this is?" She waved the paper in the air.

Gideon rose from his seat and stomped over to her. He snatched the document from her hand and read it. The skin on his neck turned splotchy and sweat dotted his brow. "Where did you get this?" Gideon demanded.

Katherine smirked. "From me. It proves you were Angela's father."

My mouth dropped open. Talk about a plot twist! I didn't see that one coming, either. But it made sense. Sofía told me that Angela's father paid for the funeral, probably out of guilt, and he lived in Mystique. This murder mystery was becoming a twisty V. C. Andrews novel. The housekeeper and the millionaire?

Katherine took a peek at the paper, then gasped. "It's a DNA assessment. I knew it!" She stepped away from Gideon and Maria until her spine hit the bar, her gaze darting between them. "You two were…lovers? I think I just threw up in my mouth."

I remembered the torn piece of paper I'd found in

Angela's apartment, the DNA paperwork. Suddenly, I had a strong hunch who the killer was.

Weatherby and Mrs. Harrington returned and hovered in the doorway. A muscle in Weatherby's jaw was twitching. Mrs. Harrington clutched a handbag.

Sofía cleared her throat and moved to a corner of the room. "Can I have everyone's attention, please? Since we're sharing truths tonight, I know who killed Angela—"

The lights went out and a gunshot resounded. A woman screamed.

CHAPTER 26

"*CHALUPA! CHALUPA!*" I SHOUTED INTO THE DARKNESS.

"Danika?" Ryker replied somewhere to my left. "Why are you yelling?"

"Chalupa!" I cried. "That was a gunshot, Ryker. Did you forget the safe word already?"

The lights flickered back on. A cloud of sulfurous and metallic smoke filled the dining room. Sofía lay in a pool of blood, shot clean through the heart.

Everyone clamored from their seats as if someone had dropped a grenade. Maria crashed to her knees next to her stepdaughter. My stomach leaped into my throat.

"Call an ambulance!" Nate bellowed. He rushed over and knelt beside Sofía. Nate took off his jacket and pressed it against the chest wound. Blood soaked the cloth.

Katherine whipped out a phone and dialed emergency services. She walked into the adjoining room, talking to the dispatcher.

The room went still and as quiet as a church during evening prayer. Cassie's hands flew up to cover her mouth. All the blood rushed from Patrick's face. Maria's expression was grim and tight, her stare fixed on her stepdaughter. Gideon seemed immobile and his chest rose and fell under labored breathing.

Weatherby and Mrs. Harrington still stood in the doorway. One of Mrs. Harrington's hands quivered at her side hidden behind the folds of her indigo blazer.

Sofia's vacant stare gazed lifelessly up at the ceiling. Her lips parted on a last exhale and her body went limp. Sofia's head lolled to the side. She was dead.

Tears quivered on my eyelids. Someone had shot Sofia. With a gun. In the chest. My heart lurched and I suddenly found it hard to breathe.

Ryker stood next to me and I leaned into his side. He draped an arm around me. His own body was trembling in shock. "Do you think Sofia knew who the killer was?" he whispered.

"No. She was going to accuse Cassie and embarrass her, but she's innocent," I said.

"Nate," Maria said, her voice low and anguished.

Nate ignored her and kept putting pressure on the wound. His eyes filled with tears.

Maria laid a hand on his arm. "You can stop now. She's gone..."

Nate leaned back and stayed beside the body. "Who did this? Who shot her?"

"Blanche did," I said.

Chairs scraped across hardwood and heads swiveled toward the kitchen doorway.

Mrs. Harrington stood perfectly still except for her trembling hand wrapped around a handgun. "If you want something done right, you have to do it yourself. I knew Sofia was blackmailing my son and I ordered Weatherby to put an end to it. But the fool bumbled the whole thing..." Her cold stare swept over the guests, lingering on me. "Now I just need to silence the rest of you" She raised the gun and pointed it at me.

Before she could fire, Ryker rushed over and knocked the weapon from her hand. It hit the floor with a thud. Mrs. Harrington lifted the hem of her dress and bolted from the room. Patrick and Ryker started to run after her, but Weatherby blocked the doorway. The three men struggled. Finally, Ryker and Patrick were able to overtake the older man and shove past him. Weatherby chased after them through the house.

"What is Grandmother talking about, Father?" Nate settled his glasses more firmly upon his nose.

Gideon swore under his breath, his hands shaking. "Sofia's been extorting money from me for months." His voice was whisper thin.

"Why would she blackmail you?" Nate asked.

"It was because of those genealogy tests your sister had us take last Christmas from that DNA company," Gideon said. "I had my suspicions that she knew the truth about…Angela, and that's why she purchased the kits."

"Because she guessed that Angela was your daughter," I said.

"Now that I think about it, they do look alike," Cassie said. "Gideon and Angela had the same eyes."

Ryker and Patrick entered the room, breathing heavily. Patrick went over to Cassie standing against the wall. Cassie was trembling and Patrick rubbed her back with one hand.

"Weatherby drove off with Mrs. Harrington before we could catch them, but I got the license plate number," Ryker said.

I faced Gideon. "That day I confronted you on the street.

You were upset over Angela's death. Did your mother find out she was your daughter and poison Angela?"

"No." Gideon's expression crumbled as he poured himself another scotch and took a gulp. He set the glass on the bar. "I think that was Weatherby's doing."

"Why kill Sofía?" Patrick asked, raking a hand through his hair.

"She was a liability," I said.

"My mother probably thought she was protecting the family from a scandal. From exposing the truth about Angela's parentage." Gideon wearily sighed. "And because Sofía started blackmailing me shortly after we got the DNA results in the mail...I- I had hidden them, or so I thought."

A feminine snicker had everyone turning toward Katherine, who had returned and sat at the table. "The police are on their way."

Gideon snapped his head in her direction, his fists clenching. "It was *you*, Katherine. Wasn't it?"

Katherine took a dainty sip of wine. "I found the DNA results in your office safe, Father. Remember last summer when I asked you for a loan to expand my business and you turned me down? Well, I couldn't get a loan anywhere else, either. So when I discovered that Angela was your daughter, I convinced Sofía to help me extort you. However, the night Angela died, Sofía and I met up at the coffee shop. Sofía wanted to stop extorting the money, and I reluctantly agreed. The next day, we heard Angela was dead."

All true. My nape stayed warm.

"That's why you lied," I said. "You weren't meeting a potential investor, but Sofía, your partner in blackmailing crime."

Katherine raised her wine glass as if in a salute. "You're smarter than you look."

The fire in the hearth was crackling and shooting sparks. The room felt too warm and stuffy.

"I was paying Sofía—*you*, five thousand dollars a month!" Gideon shouted at his daughter. "You greedy, ungrateful child."

"Oh, I'm not *that* greedy, Father," Katherine said in a casual tone. "I split the money with Sofía. She wanted to buy a townhouse, and I needed the capital to expand my business overseas. What are you complaining about anyway? Were you even paying child support to Maria? I doubt it since you wanted to keep your love child a secret from Mother." She took a sip of wine. "And besides, you make millions of dollars a year. This was loose change for you."

The deposit slip that I'd found with Sofía's name on it made sense now. That's why she had all that cash.

Cassie's cheeks were moist with tears. Patrick heaved a sigh and one hand clutched his chest. His complexion looked green as if he might throw up.

My gaze went to Maria. She sat on the floor and stared at her stepdaughter's body with a numb, dazed expression. Maria had lost two daughters now.

My heart pinched. Angela never knew her biological father was a married man living in the same town, who had paid an extortionist to keep his illegitimate child a secret and refused to even acknowledge her.

"It was all just a huge mistake," Gideon mumbled.

"*Oh!* I think I understand," I said, pacing the room. "Gideon wanted to poison Sofía, not Angela, for blackmailing him. Am I right?"

Gideon swallowed hard. He plopped onto a chair and buried his head in his hands. "I never wanted that. Weatherby took matters into his own hands on my mother's orders."

"Tell us what happened. The truth, Father," Nate said.

With his head still down, Gideon sighed. "Weatherby was following Sofía. One night he saw Angela and Sofía at the coffee shop. He told me that Patrick entered and the three of them got into an argument."

"I remember that night," Patrick said in a hushed tone. "Angela found Sofía's credit card receipt to the Sleep Inn and she threw a hissy fit."

"You mean, Angela figured out that you were having an affair with Sofía," Ryker said. "And Angela confronted you both." He glanced at Cassie, his expression contrite. "I'm sorry, I didn't mean that to come out so harsh, but you should know."

Patrick threw Ryker a vicious glare and stiffened without answering. Poor Cassie started weeping.

The credit card receipt that I'd found at Angela's apartment made even more sense now.

"I knew it!" Cassie exclaimed and glared at Patrick. "You told me I was imagining things like the stinky perfume and long brown hairs on your clothes. *Ugh!*" She punched him in the gut and he doubled over. "Patrick, I pronounce you dumped and single. You may now kiss my butt." Sniffling, Cassie strode to the far side of the room with her arms crossed.

I went over to Cassie and put my arm over her shoulders. She leaned into my side with a sniffle.

"Some men are jerks," I whispered.

Everyone was quiet a moment. I avoided looking at Sofía's body, at the blood pooling on the floor beneath her.

"Did you have Weatherby kill Angela?" Nate asked his father. "Or did Grandmother?"

Gideon shook his head numbly. "Definitely not."

"Then what happened?" I said. "Who killed Angela?"

"It was a ghastly mistake..." Gideon downed the last of

his scotch and plonked the empty glass on the table. "While Angela, Sofía, and Patrick had their backs turned, Weatherby said he slipped the poison into a red bottle on the table. He thought it belonged to Sofía since the container was next to her purse. Then Angela suddenly returned to the table and drank the tonic, yelling that Patrick would be her man now. After more quarreling, the manager kicked the three of them out of the coffee shop. Weatherby realized Angela had ingested the poison and ran out after her, but she'd already taken off."

It sounded like a twisted game of *Clue*—the butler in the coffee shop with the poisoned love tonic.

"I think I know what happened next," I said. "Angela must have sensed something was wrong after drinking the potion and went to the shop to find my grandma. Except Angela died before she could get help, and traces of the deadly plant were found on her coat because she worked at the florist." I glanced at Gideon. "But how did you get the Tanas Root?"

Gideon looked up. "Weatherby told me that he stole the plant from the florist shop. He knew which herb to take since my mother's a botanist."

Cassie sniffled. Patrick sat down heavily on a chair. Neither of them said a word.

Maria, who'd been silent until now, got to her feet. She stood over Sofía's body. Her face was blotchy red and her hard glare focused on Gideon. "You murdered our child!"

Gideon jumped to his feet and spread his arms wide in a pleading gesture. "That was *never* my intention. I swear it. Weatherby was supposed to scare Sofía, *not* kill her."

"You deserve to rot in jail," Maria spat, her voice as shrill as the whistle of a teakettle on a quiet night.

"I suppose I do," Gideon muttered. "But I never ordered

Weatherby to kill Sofia, my mother must've done that. It seems Weatherby even tried to poison Sofia again by putting the poison in her coffee at work. I had nothing to do with that, either."

Sirens wailed in the distance. The police and paramedics were on their way.

"What about the voodoo doll in Cassie's car?" I asked. "Who's responsible for that?"

Maria waved her hand, then dropped it. "After Angela died, I found the doll among her things and took it home. I knew that Patrick was responsible for leading Angela on and having an affair with Sofia. Patrick was making my daughters act like cats in heat. I had to put an end to it."

"So you tried to hex Patrick?" I said.

Maria nodded with a shrug. "I followed Patrick to the barber shop one day and after he left, I asked the hairstylist if I could have the hair to scare off the deer in our yard. The man swept up the strands and put them in a bag. Once I had Patrick's hair, I sewed it into the doll's head and put the thing in his car with a note to frighten him."

The police and paramedics burst into the room. Pandemonium ensued. The authorities put the gun into an evidence bag, then questioned everyone present. Sheriff Hall called the coroner. The next few hours were a blur, and once everybody had given their statements, Gideon was arrested and a warrant for Weatherby and Mrs. Harrington's arrest had been issued. The coroner took away the body and the forensics team did their thing.

As Deputy Reid was guiding Gideon through the house in cuffs, Nate stopped them in the entryway.

Nate inhaled sharply, then exhaled. "Father, there's something I need to tell you."

Gideon peered at his son. "Yes?"

"I promise to visit every Sunday while you're in prison," Nate said, squaring his shoulders. "And I'm gay."

Nate looked over at me and we shared a smile.

A slim woman wearing a long purple nightgown under a flimsy robe and feathery high-heeled slippers descended the staircase. Her brassy, gold-blonde hair was styled off her face and held up by a jeweled clip. The woman looked about forty-five with a smooth, unlined face and a creamy complexion. One slender hand rose to clutch the pearls at her throat.

"*Stop!* Where are you taking my husband? What is going on?"

This must've been Eleanor Harrington, Nate's mother.

"I'm sorry, ma'am, but your husband's under arrest," Deputy Reid said. "He's being charged with accessory after the fact in the death of Angela Hernández."

"This is outrageous! My husband couldn't have had anything to do with such vulgarness," Eleanor shrilled as she rushed into the entryway. "You have no proof that my husband did anything wrong."

Deputy Reid grunted. "We have a room full of people who heard his confession, ma'am. Now if you'll excuse me."

Gideon swung his head in her direction. "Honey, call our lawyer and have him meet me at the station."

"Yes, darling," Eleanor replied.

Gideon grunted as the deputy pushed him out the front door.

Eleanor stamped over to me. She stabbed a red nail in my face, and I backed up a step. "I know who you are. Blanche told me about you, Danika Dreary. This is all your fault. You talked Nathaniel into this dinner party and once again someone from your horrid family is ruining my husband's life. Like mother like daughter!"

My skin flushed and I grinded my teeth. My family was

considered upstanding citizens compared to the murderous Harrington family.

Before I could respond, Eleanor sashayed into the parlor, presumably to call their lawyer. I guess Eleanor held the same grudges as the other Harringtons.

Sheriff Robert Hall approached me. "May I have word, Danika?"

"Yeah, what's up?"

The sheriff rocked on his heels. "I told you to stay out of the investigation, but you didn't. However, what you did, inviting everyone to dinner to get to the truth was...a good call. Thank you for helping."

"Anytime, Sheriff."

"We'll talk soon." He patted my shoulder with a slight smile, then moseyed out the door.

Everyone was leaving now. I went outside to wait for Ryker by the Audi.

Ryker walked out the door, made his way over to me, and smiled. "The murder has been solved thanks to you."

Grinning, I jabbed him in the ribs with my elbow. "Gee, it was nothing. Plus, I had a handsome sidekick who helped a little."

Ryker leaned closer. "Now that we're unofficially off the case. How about I take you to dinner some time. There's a new Mexican restaurant in town—"

"You had me at tacos." I smiled wider and kissed his cheek.

CHAPTER 27
EPILOGUE

I thought I'd bring you up-to-date on the adventures of Danika Dreary, detective extraordinaire. Okay, so maybe I wasn't a real detective, or extraordinary, but Sheriff Hall did say I could be a consultant for the police department as long as I didn't go trying to solve any more crimes on my own. I might've had my fingers crossed behind my back when I agreed.

What about the Harringtons, you ask? Well, Nate was out of the closet with his family and he was going on his first date with the redheaded waiter next week. His father, Gideon, testified against Weatherby and his mother, who were apprehended the day after Mrs. Harrington shot Sofía. They were both charged with first-degree murder. Gideon was put on house arrest and continued to run his business from home. Katherine did expand her perfume business overseas with the help of her mother, Eleanor, who invested a large sum into her company.

Luis and Maria Hernández, Sofía and Angela's parents, moved out of town shortly after Sofía's funeral. She was laid to rest beside Angela. The couple relocated to Castro Valley, California, to open an ice cream parlor.

Curious about the others? Well, Cassie Peters was currently single, and Patrick Hoang wore a scarlet letter. Not actually, but he should have been forced to by the women of Mystique. However, Cassie did post flyers all over town with his picture and stated he was a no-good, lying, cheater to be avoided at all costs. I doubted he'd get many dates now. And I hoped Patrick would think twice before cheating on someone again.

Keisha Gardener was still hoping for a love match by my grandma, and continued to work part-time at Karma Moon. Me and my new bestie plan to have coffee together next week.

Which brings me to Grandma Elsie. She began matchmaking again, and realized that fixing up Nate with Angela was a sibling match, *not* a love match. She had unknowingly tried to bring two family members together and she felt sad that Angela never had a chance to get to know her half-siblings.

Curious about Sashay, the cutest, fluffiest, sweetest cat in the whole world? I might be a tad biased. You'll be happy to know that Sashay was very happy in her new home with me and Grandma Elsie. My grandma was right, Sashay and I had a special bond, and I was grateful that I got to keep her.

As you know, Ryker asked me out on an official first date. Which was absurd because I had stated numerous times that I wasn't planning on getting involved with anyone since I wasn't staying in town. I was going to be out the door faster than you could say, *cheese enchilada,* now that the murder had been solved.

Still wondering if I was going on that date with Ryker? I won't keep you in suspense: Mexican food was involved, so how could I say no?

Me? I was eating a big slice of Humble Pie ala mode. I'd been on my own most of my life and it was ingrained into my chromosomes to accomplish things by my individual merits. Not going to lie, it gave me an odd sense of achievement. While I felt it was okay to seek help when needed, I still wanted to earn the right to run a business. The only way to prove my worth was to make Mystique my permanent home and co-own Karma Moon, which was also a nice way to honor my grandma. She must've believed in me if she wanted us to own the shop together.

It was finally time to settle down and build some roots and there was no place I'd rather do that than here. And did I mention that I also joined the local book club?

"You're home now, Danika," Grandma Elsie said, patting my hand.

We sat in the living room on the sofa, with Sashay purring contently between us.

Home. A word that meant family, love, support, friendship, and security. Home was a word that held new meaning to me now.

I kissed my grandma's cheek, stroked Sashay's head, and then went to my room to get ready for my date. Hopefully, we'd have the night off from any more hexes and hijinks, but with me around, you never know...

CHAPTER 28
FREE READ!

I HAVE A FREE COZY PARA-MYSTERY NOVELLA, SPELLBOOK SECRETS!

Molly Blackwell, proud owner of Blackwell's Books and Brews, is a witch with a knack for crafting the perfect latte.

And life in the charming town of Elderberry Edge is

delightfully quaint—until the day Molly stumbles upon a cursed spellbook hidden in her cafe. Because apparently, running a business isn't challenging enough without adding a hex to the mix.

When Molly accidentally releases a mischievous ghost, her peaceful existence gets flipped faster than a magical pancake. Teaming up with her best friend Piper Holloway, a sassy ghost-whisperer, Molly sets out to restore order and salvage her Yelp reviews.

Now, Molly and Piper must expose a killer, break an ancient curse, and convince their new spectral friend that haunting isn't a valid career choice. All before Molly has to add 'Haunted Barista' to her resumé.

Can Molly and Piper solve the mystery in time, or will the ghostly pranks haunt Elderberry Edge forever?

Join my newsletter to get your free eBook: https://BookHip.com/BZHCWMP

CHAPTER 29
HUMBLE REQUEST

Dear Awesome Reader,

Can I tell you a secret? The best way to keep a book series alive isn't found in any tarot reading—it's the magic of reader support! If you enjoyed spending time in Mystique with Danika and her quirky crew, I'd be thrilled if you'd leave an honest review online.

And if you know someone who loves cozy mysteries as much as you do, sharing this story with them would make my cat's day and mine!

Reviews and recommendations are like magical ingredients in a love potion—each one helps the series grow stronger. But even if reviews aren't your cup of tea, I wanted to thank you for choosing to spend your precious reading time with my characters. Your support means the world to me.

With gratitude and pixie dust,
~Sherry

CHAPTER 30
ALL HALLOWS HOMICIDE

WITH A PASSION FOR SPELLCRAFT AND ALL THINGS macabre, Penelope Primrose spends her days hexing dust bunnies and haggling over haunted hatboxes at her curio shop, Thirteen Treasures.

But her All Hallows' Eve party goes from spooktacular to

spectacularly wrong when a shady antique dealer ends up dead. And nobody ruins her favorite holiday and gets away with it!

Armed with her snarky feline familiar, Malarkey, and more determination than a ghost with unfinished business, Penelope vows to crack the case. But solving the mystery isn't as simple as waving a wand. The distractingly handsome sheriff keeps giving her side-eye, and the suspects are more colorful than a bag of Halloween candy.

Between cursed teacups, menacing craft projects, and danger lurking around every headstone, she'll need all her wit and whimsy to catch a killer before they strike again. Because in Scarecrow Springs—where even the ravens have secrets—nothing is quite what it seems.

Can this charmingly optimistic witch solve the case, or will this Halloween haunt her forever?

you like witchy heroines, furry-talking sidekicks, and a dash of romance, then you'll love this delightful whodunit.

START READING YOUR COPY TODAY!

CHAPTER 31
BOOKED FOR MURDER

A bewitching bookstore. A tome of secrets. And a crime-solving witch.

AFTER INHERITING A MAGICAL BOOKSHOP AND AN obnoxious black cat, Mercy Brew moves to Hemlock Hills,

California, with her French bulldog. For a bibliophile witch, it's a dream come true.

Unfortunately, the bookstore also comes with a murder mystery to solve.

When Mercy discovers that her eccentric aunt was murdered and an irate coven member turns up dead, she knows trouble is brewing. Especially when Mercy becomes the prime suspect in the crimes, and both casualties are linked to a mystically sealed book.

Determined to clear her name, Mercy enlists the help of a gorgeous werewolf and two quirky witches. But in a seaside town where secrets bubble like witch's brew, Mercy could be the killer's next target.

START READING YOUR COPY TODAY!

About the Author

Sherry Soule writes amusing, action-packed, and character-driven cozy para-mysteries, supernatural mysteries, paranormal romances, and urban fantasy for both YA and adult readerships. Many of her books have been on the Amazon bestseller lists and nominated as top picks in the "Best Paranormal Romance" categories on numerous review sites.

Currently, Sherry lives in Northern California with her family, and four to six spoiled rescue cats. She is an enthusiast of Disneyland, Victorian mansions, coffee, Halloween, and saving stray felines. Sherry will deny that she has a serious book addiction, which she firmly believes isn't hoarding if it's filling a bookshelf.

Psst, reader. Yeah, you, subscribe to Sherry's newsletter to be notified of new releases and freebies, so she can feed her growing army of cats: http://eepurl.com/L4UyD

Places you can find Sherry online:
Author Amazon Profile (Follow me!)
Official Author Blog
And visit me on Sherry Facebook Page

Acknowledgments

A huge thank you and lots of love to these fellow writers and friends who helped me revise this book: Andrea R. Cooper, Lisa Bouchard, and Carmen Erickson. You are bestest writing buddies a girl could ask for!

Made in the USA
Coppell, TX
23 January 2025